A. ZOYA

ZAZI

First published by DADYMINDS PUBLISHERS INSIDER 2024

Copyright © 2024 by A. Zoya

All rights reserved. No part of this publication may be reproduced, stored or transmitted in any form or by any means, electronic, mechanical, photocopying, recording, scanning, or otherwise without written permission from the publisher. It is illegal to copy this book, post it to a website, or distribute it by any other means without permission.

This novel is entirely a work of fiction. The names, characters and incidents portrayed in it are the work of the author's imagination. Any resemblance to actual persons, living or dead, events or localities is entirely coincidental.

A. Zoya asserts the moral right to be identified as the author of this work.

A. Zoya has no responsibility for the persistence or accuracy of URLs for external or third-party Internet Websites referred to in this publication and does not guarantee that any content on such Websites is, or will remain, accurate or appropriate.

Designations used by companies to distinguish their products are often claimed as trademarks. All brand names and product names used in this book and on its cover are trade names, service marks, trademarks and registered trademarks of their respective owners. The publishers and the book are not associated with any product or vendor mentioned in this book. None of the companies referenced within the book have endorsed the book.

Learn more about the DADYMINDS Company: https://www.dadyminds.org.

The Publisher: DPG (DADYMINDS PUBLISHING GROUP) is the subsidiary trademark in charge of book publishing and author services at DADYMINDS HOLDINGS LLC. (Discover more via: https://publishing.dadyminds.org)

Imprint: DPI (DADYMINDS PUBLISHERS INSIDER)

Email: publishing@dadyminds.org

WhatsApp: +250 (781) 355-361/+1 (307) 323-4616

Mail: 1007 North Orange Street, 4th Floor Suite #2987, Wilmington, Delaware, United States

Second edition

ISBN (paperback): 979-8-3493-1550-3
ISBN (hardcover): 979-8-30-889143-7

Editing by Anath Lee Wales

This book was professionally typeset on Reedsy.
Find out more at reedsy.com

Dedicated to all my fans, readers and for everyone who love me, I love you too.

"In this tale of drama involving unreliable parents, broken friendships, and disloyalty—a life where dreams are built only to be shattered. Growing up too quickly, Zazi learns that life's twists and turns often come with harsh lessons: be careful what you wish for."

From the Author: A. Zoya

Contents

Reader's Invitation	ii
Prologue	1
Introduction	3
1 Hollow Beginning	8
2 Breaking Point	17
3 Fragile Connections	27
4 Price of Escape	32
5 A New Kind of Hurt	39
6 Carrying the Weight	48
7 Cost of Betrayal	56
8 Family Ties and Fault Lines	64
9 Crossroads of Choice	71
10 Forgiveness as Liberation	80
11 Whisper of Hope	88
12 Facing the Ruins	100
13 Knowing Thyself	108
Epilogue	115
About the Author	117

Reader's Invitation

Dear Reader,

Welcome to the world of ZAZI.

This is more than merely a story—a journey through resilience, heartbreak, and the unyielding pursuit of self-discovery. Zazi's path is fraught with challenges that may resonate all too well, yet her strength and determination remind us that hope can illuminate even the darkest moments.

I invite you to contemplate your narrative as you turn the pages. What storms have you weathered? How have you discovered strength when it felt impossible?

Your voice is essential, and I would love to hear your thoughts. Let us continue this conversation together:

Share your thoughts and favourite moments on social media with **#Zazi-Knows**.

Feel free to connect with me directly at [Insert Email Address].

Thank you for choosing to walk alongside Zazi. I hope her story resonates with you as profoundly as it has with me.

With gratitude,
   A. Zoya

Prologue

When love is lost, and the self fades into shadows, which do you seek first? Can you discover love without understanding yourself, or must you piece together your identity before love arrives? Perhaps neither is truly found; instead, both must be created, forged from the fragments of a life that refuses to shatter entirely.

This is Zazi's story. She is a girl thrust into a world of uncertainty, shaped by the absence of those meant to guide her. Raised by individuals who tried but failed to fill the void, she grew up within the cracks of family, trust, and belonging. Love felt like an unanswered question, whilst her identity resembled a puzzle with missing pieces.

Her journey is betrayal, broken dreams, crumbling friendships and fading loyalties. It tells a tale in which wishes frequently bring consequences, and every glimmer of hope appears wrapped in sorrow. For Zazi, life was an unrelenting storm, tearing through everything she believed she knew and compelling her to reconstruct herself repeatedly.

But even storms possess their tranquil moments. Amidst the chaos, there is space for discovery. What does accepting a life that offers both beauty and brutality mean? What does it entail to grow, not despite the pain, but as a result of it?

This tale is not a fantasy; instead, it is filled with riddles—the kind that life presents us with when we least expect them. It is not a fairy tale, yet there is magic in Zazi's strength and unyielding hope, which see her through even the darkest nights.

Zazi learns a most challenging lesson through heartbreak and horror: acceptance is not surrender. It is not standing still in the face of defeat but finding the courage to move forward, to dream once more, even when dreams have turned to ash.

Her story is one of endings and beginnings, falling and rising, losing herself and finding something greater. In every shattered moment, she discovers a new piece of herself, a more profound truth about what it means to know oneself—and to believe in the possibility of love once more.

Introduction

The novel Zazi tells the story of a girl raised by her grandparents after her parents abandoned her. While her father never showed any interest in her life, her mother disappeared without a trace or a word when she was just about yay-high.

Due to this, she led a very difficult, lonely, empty, and hollow life, believing that something was missing. She could not quite understand why she felt that way because her grandparents gave her everything and more. Well, maybe not everything, as they couldn't give her emotional support, love, or affection like a normal child. They always threw money at her and used hurtful words to "toughen her up," which made her wonder, "Had my parents raised me, would the treatment—or lack thereof—be the same? Would it be worse? Better? What if?" So, now and then, she would pray and wish that her parents would somehow fall from the sky. Had she known that when they did—or at least one of them did—all hell would break loose, she probably would have reconsidered those wishes and prayers...

The other thing that bothered her was how she lived in the same house as her aunts and uncles but only had a relationship with a few of them as if her uncle Maurice (Mo) and her aunt Tamara refused to acknowledge her existence. They never spoke to her and treated her like a stranger—the stranger is too kind; it was more like she was the enemy. She thought, "He probably doesn't like me because I'm his biological niece."

Maurice was not her grandfather's child, nor was her grandmother, who raised her mother's biological mother... So, the grandmother who raised her was her step-grandmother, and Uncle Maurice was her grandfather's stepson. They didn't get along very well, and Maurice often caused trouble and didn't understand how that was a problem...

Zazi's life appeared perfect in the eyes of the stranger, yet most people couldn't understand why she still longed for her parents' return. After all, why would anyone want people who didn't want them? Perhaps what truly mattered was understanding "why they didn't want her." She needed to know, but she couldn't answer those questions herself. Additionally, constantly being surrounded by friends and peers who talked about their parents was incredibly uncomfortable, as she could never relate and could not respond to the curious questions, which always revolved around, "Why don't you ever talk about your parents? Why do you always mention your grandparents?"

It was a lot for her because saying things like "which, hey abandoned me, they didn't want me or think I was worth keeping..." These words left a bitter taste in her mouth...

She was forced to accept things and probably be more grateful... Now, she just had to make herself believe that her parents were gone.

But as soon as she began to accept and believe that her mum would return, she felt pleased—until she didn't...

Her mother returned, causing chaos, and it was certainly not a beautiful mess. Next, she found herself in Cape Town at a stranger's door—a furious-looking man who wasn't aware of or particularly pleased about her presence...

That whole night turned into a tragedy where her innocence was ripped off and taken brutally without her consent, but then again, she hadn't even reached the age of consent. She was but a 9-year-old...

Introduction

She had never been so terrified in her life or traumatised, but who was she going to tell? Her newfound mum? Who she hadn't seen since they arrived in Cape Town? The unwelcoming husband she didn't even know was married to her mum? No, she couldn't tell anyone. She had to keep to herself. Besides, who would believe her? After all, she had watched so many films where the girl is always to blame and is never seen or treated like the perpetrator... The abuse continued for the two years she lived there, having to listen to the sounds of her mum being beaten at night while the rest of the house slept like babies as if nothing was happening. But I suppose it happened so often it became the norm... This behaviour was new to Zazi; she had only seen it on television. Witnessing it in real life was overwhelming... Moreover, downgrading from suburban life to living in a shack was a lot to process... The township was filled with maniacs, lacking peace or quiet, rife with domestic and gang violence, gunshots every other night... Watching the community take matters into their own hands, witnessing murder and violence almost every other week, every night before she closed her eyes, she could see their eyes as they took their last breath and felt guilty... Or did she believe there was a better way until she was led to think otherwise...

Facing scrutiny, humiliation, and mockery from her peers in the streets for things beyond her control, she felt as though she had been thrown to the wolves and abandoned by her mother to be devoured. This led her to grow up with a great deal of anger, which she directed at her younger sister, the spitting image of their father, the husband.

Dealing with Byron's abuse—physical, verbal, and sexual—both in private and among his friends... He relished showing off.

Then came a time in 2014 when her grandma called, and she was glad she could return to Queenstown because living in Cape Town felt like a never-ending nightmare. She thought going home would resolve everything... It did for a while, but she was no longer that innocent child. A lot had changed. She was constantly feeling frisky. She had become accustomed to being made to watch porn, and she didn't know how to cope. She was ashamed, disgusted with herself, and terrified... Things with Tamara still hadn't changed, nor had they with Maurice; her grandparents also treated her differently... She and her grandfather were no longer as close, and they didn't talk much due to what she might say to him. He had also grown meaner over the years...

When Amanda and Anton came to live with them, things escalated further at home. Shend and Amanda got along well, but it felt like Amanda and Tamara were ganging up on her at times. Seeing how close the twins were to Tamara was heartbreaking, as Shend wondered what she had done to her aunt that made her hate her so much...

Returning home was terrific, but a great deal had changed. She grew closer to her grandmother than she did to her grandfather. Tamara had a baby, and the twins (Amanda and Anton) moved in. We had different nannies every other month, and for some reason, they never got along with Zazi; it felt like they were weapons formed against her. Although she was grateful Anton was always there for her—so caring and thoughtful—he consistently stood up for her and protected her like a big brother. It was nice because no one ever fought for her; she had to fight for herself. However, she hated that it seemed as though she was driving a wedge between the twins. Zazi's grandmother's relatives now had a more significant reason to visit because of Amanda and Anton. Zazi had nothing against them, but it always felt like they loathed her, excluded her, and didn't like her—a sentiment she never understood. Sometimes, she wished she could speak to someone. Her grandfather was no help, and everyone else was a lost cause. She would miss her Aunt Thelma, as she could confide in her, but she also lacked a phone or her number and was forbidden from mentioning her name...

She never understood why, while her grandma behaved as if they were the problem when they weren't. Family politics and drama were one thing Zazi despised, and she consistently found herself caught in the midst of it all, compelled to choose a side.

Introduction

Hence, she concentrated on school and attempted to enjoy herself there until it ceased to be enjoyable and was no longer a haven. She was bullied, and everyone seemed to be on her case. Most people appeared intimidated or annoyed by her presence, and she never understood why…

She began to act out. Now a teenager, she remained obedient and respectful; however, people like her grandmother, Amanda, the nannies, and even her peers at school continued to provoke her. She endeavoured to maintain her composure until she could no longer do so at home, where everyone deemed her a disrespectful child, peculiar, or thought something was amiss. In truth, something was wrong. She had been forced to grow up far too quickly and was traumatised, yet at the time, she was unaware that she still did not know whether she could discuss it. She could sense that she had lost herself and continued to lose herself… She attempted to calm herself and discern what was troubling her, but it felt overwhelming. She concealed all that pain within a box and embraced it… She could scarcely recognise herself anymore. Thus, the title "ZAZI", which means Know Thyself, reflects her journey to understand herself better…

One

Hollow Beginning

"Home is not merely a place; at times, it's the love you yearn for but never discover."

"The lack of love creates a void, but the lack of self produces a silence that resonates endlessly."

On a day of serpentines, bourbon, wine, and dining, how can one ever discern what is acceptable and what is not? Carrot chips put her at bitter odds.

They said the home was the place to be, yet she was uncertain where that was or how it should feel, being a discarded bundle.

The woman meant to be her mother fled before she could wake. Though only four years old, she was confident the night before would be the last time she saw her; she had never known her father.

She was raised by her grandparents. Her elderly relatives were terrific, though she sometimes wished she had been more honest with herself. She felt as if she was ungrateful. They endeavoured to fill the void; perhaps they believed they had, but it never felt sufficient.

At school, she always had friends with something to say about their parents, but her mother's image gradually faded.

She had even convinced her younger self that she was dead. I mean, nobody ever spoke of her, not even a whisper.

So she had to look ahead rather than dwell on the past, although she couldn't help but contemplate what life might have been like had her ancestors been present.

She had already painted a picture of what life might have been like—well, in her head, of course... life, hm... Little did she know, someone ought to have warned her.

Do you know what they say about *being cautious with one's wishes? Oh, well, she ought to have* heeded that advice...

It was a Saturday morning, and everyone appeared cheerful. She was curious about why.

Walking down to the kitchen, she was taken aback to find only her aunt and uncle preparing breakfast, so she joined them and helped.

Just as they were preoccupied, the doorbell rang. Her uncle and aunt rushed to the door, grinning widely. They appeared somewhat ridiculous, but she couldn't resist laughing. Driven by curiosity, she followed suit and approached the front door. After taking two more steps, she suddenly halted. Shocked and in disbelief, she couldn't believe her eyes, and without thinking, she dashed into her arms as if the wind were propelling her. Her face may have been blurry moments ago, but this particular visage was undeniably familiar; she recognised her from somewhere... oh! Yes, and if her memory served her right, this was meant to be her mother. However, as the excitement faded from her eyes, she immediately withdrew upon seeing what she had brought with her. Zazi couldn't help but feel disgusted as she set her offspring down.

She wasn't confident whether it was hatred or anger that she felt. All she knew was that she simply wished to strangle the life out of that infant.

The next thing she knew, she felt obliged to play the big sister.

Her supposed mother seemed nice for a minute or two as they baked and cooked together, not even bothered by the small talk. Yet, she dreaded having a tail on her back every second. "Watch the child; she wants to bond with you."

"Bond my left foot," she thought, but not aloud, as she rolled her eyes in utter irritation. Enough was enough; she couldn't behave like her mother, and her brat didn't just hijack her life after vanishing for years and never looking back. Now, she's returned without notice to play pretend while pretending to be the mother of the year to her little brat, knowing full well that she had cast her aside. How was poor little Zazi supposed to feel?

Despite Zazi's frustration, there was a ceremony outside, so she needed to compose herself as she stepped out for a breather.

There were raucous noises and a throng of people, like an Eminem concert.

And my goodness! She couldn't feel any less overwhelmed.

Anxiety crept in on her like an unpleasant rash.

As she walked out, minions gathered around her like bees. The next thing she knew, she was a Sunday school teacher, handing out biscuits like Jesus. She broke the bread, and like good little servants, they feasted. With Sunday school before her, she pondered, "Shall I preach? Shall I ditch? Oh! Lord, what to do?"

Just as she was about to leap some M.I.A. (missing in action) away from the anxiety surrounding her, she heard someone yelling.

"Zazi! Put your dress on; it's your great-grandmother's funeral, for heaven's sake; where do you think you're going?!"

This woman had no sense of timing. How many more of these insufferable moments could a girl endure, she pondered to herself...

"Nowhere!" she replied.

Woman: Very well, go and bathe and see the guests. We don't have all day, but service will commence shortly.

The woman spoke as though Zazi were running the service or cared in the slightest, as she did not want to be there.

Zazi: Yes, ma'am!

Woman: Well, off you go then.

Off she went, hurrying inside as if the wind was propelling her.

Huh! Should I not say she loathed every moment of it? The house was packed entirely as she searched for an empty room to bathe in, and to her surprise, she could not find one.

Great-aunt: What are you searching for?

Zazi: A vacant room for bathing

Great aunt: there isn't one, so just pick a room and bath. We are all females here.

Zazi: I can't bathe in front of these strangers.

Great aunt: Well, please don't, but do stop pacing to and fro. You're getting on my nerves.

So, she went to the other house to see if she could find an empty room there, preferably her grandparents' room. However, even there, the rooms were occupied. Thus, she followed her great aunt's suggestion and chose a less crowded room. She bathed and donned a white T-shirt, navy trousers, and stylish casual trainers. She arranged her hair into a lovely bun.

She tidied the room and stepped outside, but as soon as she did, trouble arose…

Voice: and then?

Zazi: what?

Voice: why are you in pants?

Zazi: I don't understand your question

Voice: It's a funeral, and you are a woman, not a man, so please wear a skirt or a dress…

And just like that, her confidence and self-esteem vanished; they soared away.

At this point, poor Zazi was fuming. She could not comprehend why everyone was harassing her instead of focusing on the funeral, which was the reason they had come to her. As she returned to the house, she bumped into her so-called mother.

Mom: what's wrong?

Zazi: nothing

Mom: talk to me

Zazi: I was yelled at for wearing trousers and instructed to wear a dress since I am female.

Mom: That's nonsense. You're not the only woman here wearing trousers. My advice? Simply ignore that person and wear whatever you fancy.

She nodded and went inside to change, as she didn't want any more trouble. She was still shocked by Veronica's advice; that was the most brilliant thing she had said since her arrival.

She decided to stop overthinking, put on a skirt, and went out to continue with her "duties" as she chuckled her way to the tent.

Voice: You can see how lovely that dress looks on you; you now appear both intelligent and perfect.

She smiled as she thought that if she opened her mouth, something vile would pop out; she felt so uncomfortable, and given her dislike for funerals, it didn't help the situation. To her, they seemed unnecessary; thus, she made it her mission to escape at any opportunity. Yes, escape; after all, she had been dragged here. After a period of lurking, she noticed that no one was watching. People appeared busy, engrossed in their affairs rather than hers, so she slowly ran back to the house, sneaked off the skirt, put on her trousers, and quickly made her way to the gate and went out. Although she wasn't quite sure where to go or what to do, everyone, including her mates and cousins, was still at the funeral. She took a stroll, but to her surprise, she saw some of her cousins playing football as she walked. Hence, she decided to join them; she did love football. It was her favourite sport, and playing football seemed appealing, but then the drama faded.

They played for a while; time must have flown by, for they noticed their belles weeping as they dragged each other, staggering back to the house. Zazi, on the other hand, had almost forgotten her anxiety until she confronted the gate in her yard. Suddenly, she couldn't breathe; her lips dried as quickly as the wind whipped up the dust, and she was back to feeling repulsed and annoyed. She felt somewhat like a raging lunatic; it must have been hunger.

They opened the gate and walked side by side. Everyone grabbed the first plate they could find, and before she—she alone—encountered trouble…
Voice 2 :Zazi! Zazi! Zazi!
"Oh my goodness, what is it now?" she thought silently.
Zazi: yes?
Voice 2: Where have you been? The funeral was nearly over, and you were nowhere to be found.
Zazi: I apologise. I stepped outside for some fresh air and lost track of the time…
Zazi detested lying, but at this stage, it was either that or facing an angry outburst.
Voice 2: Right, quickly, before they close up your great-grandmother's grave, as she pushed her towards the half-closed burial.

And all Zazi could think about was the list of better things she could have been doing with her time instead of this. I mean, she loved her great-grandmother, but she was already dead, and people were acting as if she was still dying, whereas the woman was gone and would never come back. Somewhere beneath the rage, she wished she could remember something other than the fact that she was bedridden and that Grandpa thought it was time to ship her off to a nursing home; she forced her weary feet forward, and honestly, she wasn't confident what to do with her living body, which felt already on the verge of joining the grave. Everyone hovered around her as if she was about to cry or was heartbroken when she was merely thinking back to when they had just returned from East London.

Sitting at the kitchen table, her grandfather yelled out in distress over her preferences.
Grandpa: Mom is dead
Uncle: Huh?
Grandpa: Yes! I just received a call from my sister; she's passed away.

Everyone else was in awe, but Zazi wasn't sure how to respond. Although she could see the pain in my grandfather's eyes as he continued to speak, she wasn't sure how to react.

"Well, she was quite old and hardly alive anymore, so this death is no tragedy but rather a relief."

"Huh! Funny! What a way to comfort oneself, mate," she thought.

She wanted to hug him, as what she saw on his face wasn't his most flattering look. However, she felt somewhat too exhausted, so instead, she decided to lie in her room, burying herself in her pillow.

Oh! And good heavens! She wasn't crying, merely a bit sad that her grandfather was in pain. This was somewhat surprising news to be delivered as they marched through the door; he didn't even wait for them to be seated, let alone greet them. So she was still utterly shocked, but then again, people do die, don't they?

Well, the funeral concluded, and I was prepared to head home.

At this point, Zazi wanted to return to Queenstown and get into bed, but her so-called mother had to create drama. The next thing Zazi knew, she was on a stranger's doorstep in Cape Town. It was not how she had initially arrived; everything had become blurry as if she had just been kidnapped.

It was late; evidently, they had already had supper, so everyone retired to bed in a house full of strangers without any introductions.

Zazi had no space here, as she was forced to share a bed with a stranger—a man she didn't even know, who was older than her. She was meant to be sleeping that night and during the following nights, but the man never gave her any respite. He touched her, and her innocence was lost.

She was now a minor transformed into a wife overnight, introduced to adultery, with the man performing marital rights upon her. Where was God to lift her, working overtime in the night and weeping in the morning?

Meanwhile, her so-called mother was someone she barely ever saw; she never even dared to mention that she had decided to tie the knot with a boxer who treated her like a punching bag and damned her now and then. Violence was foreign to Zazi; it was never her scene. She had only seen it in films; this was quite traumatic for her, but her so-called mother did not care, as they never even spoke nor saw each other again while her husband and nephew bossed her about.

When everyone went to bed, Zazi was compelled to watch what was believed to be in the blue films. "That's how you bend over," he would preach.

The bloke even exploited her for his better friends and compelled them to date one of the mates just so he could hit and mistreat her, yet she still had to keep an eye out for her beloved sister, and she couldn't despise her any less despite everything. She also had to adapt to a decline in her life.

I transformed from a cheese-loving girl to a fragile little thing marked by poverty and abuse.

Every weekend, they had to clean, and Byron wouldn't lift a finger but bring his friends over so he could beat and humiliate her in front of them.

So, as usual, Victoria was nowhere to be seen on this particular Saturday. She left her troublesome child for Zazi to look after, although Byron was also present; it never seemed to make much difference.

Byron would invite his friends over as usual, and then he would choose to show off and demonstrate his strength.

He got up to make his and his friend's food. Zazi hadn't eaten either, so she got up too in means to prepare food for herself…when he poured a cup of boiling water on her chest, she gasped in pain as he continued to slap and kick her.

Byron: Why must you always mimic everything I do?
Zazi: Seriously? You've just burned me.
Byron: Shut up! You do not talk when I talk
He laughed; you'd swear they were at a comedy show.

Byron: You are not going to eat until my friends and I are done.
Zazi: but I'm hungry…

Before she could finish, he slapped her again and said, "I told you not to speak, now get out of my sight," though he called her back and insisted she prepare food for them.

She felt angry, hurt, and in pain, pondering what she had done to deserve such treatment. Could it be that she harboured unfounded dislike for her mother's child? She posed questions to herself that she might never answer.

They ate, played video games, and made a mess of the whole house before leaving as he commanded.
Byron: "When I return, I want this place to be clean."

She never paused to question how deeply Victoria loved and admired him or whether she ever truly loved her. Her attempts to disregard her existence revealed all the answers.

At home, Zazi, her husband, and her child would shop for something for everyone else. It didn't bother Zazi anymore. Oh, how she wished it did, though. Every day at school, her friends would ask, "Are you okay?" She never knew how or what to answer because where would she begin?

Two

Breaking Point

"When innocence is stripped away, the world shifts, compelling one to grow in ways that one ought never to."

"Innocence is a fragile light, effortlessly taken yet profoundly missed when darkness becomes the norm."

And so another Saturday morning arrived. Zazi was sleeping so soundly and peacefully when she was suddenly suffocated in her sleep. She tried to move and get some air, but the blankets were too heavy to remove, and her body wouldn't budge. She wished to scream, but for what purpose? No one was coming to her aid. She then began to hear voices and laughter. There was a lot of muttering, but one distinctive voice said, "Give us what we want, and you can do it willingly, or we can simply take it."

The poor child didn't want to die, and even if she did, suffocating was certainly no perfect send-off in her eyes; she didn't even have to agree. They just began pulling and scratching, and she didn't have the energy to fight off a mob as they queued for it as if it were something special, like a PlayStation at a game shop.

Not knowing what to do and feeling excruciating pain, both physically and emotionally, she simply wished for it all to disappear. Her body seemed to shut down as she tried to close her eyes to avoid seeing what was happening to her; she found herself zoning in and out. Nevertheless, one bloke's intentions were unclear—whether he felt pity, didn't want to be involved, or had another reason for his words.

"I don't want to do this."

Zazi: then why are you here, David?

David: Byron compelled us to do so. I don't wish to hurt you, but we can remain here and act like I am…

Before he could finish, the door swung open, making a squeaky sound as it banged against the wardrobe. BOOM!! Another came in as he unzipped his pants, looking like he had been waiting for this moment his entire life. She could already see the thirst and excitement in his eyes as he left his pants at the door with his doing bouncing up and down. What a sight for sore eyes. Zazi wanted to throw up as she closed her eyes, rightly clenching her teeth and but cheeks, holding onto the sheets like her life depended on that grip, or maybe it did; her body went numb and unconscious. She must have passed out. A few minutes later, she woke up to a defining silence as if the house had been evacuated, so she climbed down the bed, picking up her pieces of clothing one by one in shame as if she had done something wrong when she was the one wronged, then why was she so disgusted with herself, living in self loathe, couldn't even look at her reflection she wanted to cry but what was the use? What was done was done, and they could be back anytime, and she couldn't afford to seem weak. Days passed, and nothing was better or seemed to get better. It was the same old abuse and torture over and over again.

On this particular evening, she visited Victoria's friend's house. To her surprise, her mother was there as well, so she went and sat down. She was famished, so the friend served her something her mother never did.

They were seated and appeared to be enjoying a lovely time. Then, in the blink of an eye, it was dark outside.

Next, Zazi's stepfather storms in, demanding that Victoria leave with him immediately. However, Victoria doesn't flinch as he tries to drag her, yet she remains reluctant. Instead, he grabs their child and throws her over his shoulder. As he strides out the door, he casts a look at them with murderous rage in his eyes. As he sweeps out, he storms as he walks in.

As the sound of his boots began to fill the air, peewee! He was gone, or at least they thought so, while they were still shocked and puzzled by what had just happened, debating how much of a lunatic Victoria's husband, Bongile, had suddenly appeared. The room fell quiet and darkened under the shadow of what looked like the undertaker intruding, clad in a long coat that hugged him from the neck down to the ankles. He appeared unsteady for someone who hadn't seemed so drunk just minutes before; he was quick to succumb to that liquor. His voice and tone had shifted, becoming more aggressive and violent than earlier, as he dragged himself in, yelling, "Victoria, let's go!"

Victoria: I'm not going anywhere

Bongile: either you come by yourself, or I'll drag you out of here. It's your choice.

Victoria: Did you not hear me the first time I said I wasn't going anywhere?

Bongile started pulling her by the hair, shocking everyone in awe. Zazi often heard their arguments and fights, but she had never seen them in action, much less her mother being dragged by the hair through the streets.

Victoria screamed as her friends attempted to assist, but Bongile was too strong.

Victoria: so this is why you took your daughter, so she wouldn't have to see what a monster her beloved father is? Of course, it suddenly dawned on Zazi. He took his daughter and left her to witness the trauma and monster he could become because who was she? She was not his flesh and blood;

therefore, he couldn't care less.

Margaret, my great-aunt, ran into the streets screaming, "Help, help us, please! He is going to kill my child!"

You would think that people, or at least the men who gathered to watch this as if it were entertaining, would be manly enough to tell their brothers how this was no way to treat a woman. Yet, no, they just stood there like statues, watching as Bongile dragged Victoria through the streets, and she couldn't feel more embarrassed on both sides.

He wasn't just beating and dragging her, trying to slaughter her with a machete, but slandering Victoria's name, saying she was having an affair, knowing fully well that she moved out and left him because she chose to go back to his ex, never mind go back but brought her to his house while they still lived there talk about shameless.

He continued to drag her as Victoria attempted to fend him off. Although Zazi's mind urged her to pick up a brick and strike him on the head until he became unconscious, she found herself unable to move. Instead, she stood there in a trance, mortified by her peers who had come to comfort her while tears streamed down her cheeks uncontrollably, one after another.

Victoria freed herself from Bongile's grip. She kicked him to the curb and ran into her friend's garden. Bongile shamelessly followed her inside until her friend's husband restrained him by the neck and threw him out. Bongile exclaimed, "Not in my garden or front of my children; don't disrespect me."

With his Cowardly self wiping his face with his hand, he stood to his knees with a vengeful look at Victoria, screaming, "We shall meet again, "as he walked away, swearing he would finish what he started. So no, Victoria was bleeding people in panic as she needed to be rushed to a hospital, so her uncle was called. He drove them to the hospital in the middle of the night. I don't know what was wrong with the other hospitals, but they kept skipping most of the time as if they weren't even there. Zazi was so deep inside her, thinking how her mom could have died and been murdered in front of her and how much her sister's father, Belonging, angered her. She had never felt this kind of rage before, and for an 11-year-old, it was abnormal. In the waiting area, they were waiting for word from the doctors to come and check on her, but they were all said to be rather busy while Victoria was bleeding everywhere and in pain; patients who just walked in while we sat for an hour rushed to the ER they looked terrifying.

One was in a wheelchair, and he looked as if he were burning from the inside. It was a suicide attempt gone wrong, as he fed himself paraffin, thinking it would kill him, but instead, it led him to a hospital; he appeared to be a first-rate lunatic! Zazi thought as they sat watching people being driven through. Others even resembled biltong in human flesh. It was terrifying; finally, after a couple of hours, they took Victoria. Her uncle would register her details at the reception, which was empty when they arrived; it seemed that tonight was all hands on deck. Medical licence or not, Zazi was trying to distract her mind, as she couldn't shake the thought of her mother dying. Fortunately for her, it was just a cut on her knee, so they stitched it up, gave her some painkillers, and she was discharged.

Zazi was so out of it that she couldn't remember going home that night or what happened afterwards, as her memory was foggy.

All she remembered was that it was before the event.

Victoria had acquired a new place and couldn't say it was better, at least not for Zazi. After a few weeks, Victoria's uncle and wife arrived, seeking a place to stay. Zazi often wondered why they had to pack and leave in such haste, abandoning their previous home and what had occurred in their lives that had brought them here.

Of course, Victoria, being Victoria, decided that they could live here with her, Zazi, and Zara. Somehow, Zazi knew it was a terrible idea, but no one ever listened to her, as she was a child and therefore knew nothing. For a while, it seemed and felt nice. It even felt like an actual home, although it was perhaps a bit too perfect or, better yet, a little too good to be true.

Although Victoria's uncle's wife, Lethu, did a lot for Zazi, Victoria never ironed her uniform or prepared and packed her lunch. They had decent meals, and for the first time, Zazi wasn't even the one cooking until Lethu began arguing with someone. However, it was never clear whether it was with Victoria or her husband, and suddenly, it felt like a war zone, marked by a no-trespassing sign. When Victoria couldn't afford groceries, they would go hungry as her uncle and his wife ate without concern for their hunger since they weren't in the same house. Victoria remained silent, and honestly, Zazi couldn't comprehend how she managed to endure such chaos in her own home, though after a time, they disappeared without leaving a note. Zazi, on the other hand, found herself tending to her mother's wounds, which must have been a week or two after the incident that landed Victoria in hospital.

Zazi had to take care of her, which was bad enough, considering she wasn't the best person to be around, not to mention how much of a crybaby she was. Zazi had to constantly apply pressure on the wound for it to heal quickly, massaging the leg as well, even though Victoria wouldn't allow her to finish since she would suddenly start screaming, cursing and swearing, which was annoying because Zazi didn't have to help her. Victoria was a problematic person to look after, along with her little offspring; when she thought Zazi was failing to care for hers, she suggested calling Byron for "assistance." It was even more irritating that she trusted him over Zazi. Still, at the same time, Zazi didn't care much. After all, she and her brat weren't her responsibility. Yet Zazi couldn't help but feel sorry for her in this particular state, although it wasn't long until she was back on her feet; she was never home, as usual. Zazi continued babysitting, cleaning and cooking; she was just 11 then.

She was an 11-year-old who was trauma-hounded, so if she wasn't playing Nanny McPhee, she was at the game shop called Big Daddy, where she spent most of her time and pennies. She dreaded going there as there was this particular guy who continuously preyed on her, named Dwayne, who never let her play in peace as he would always call her outside. He would lure her inside this particular cottage just behind Big Daddy all the time; he would start caressing her, shoving his tongue down her and ordering her to "take off your pants and on your knees."

He was taller, more muscular, older, and violent, so she did as she was told. "Every day after school, you will meet me here at the same time, in the same place." She couldn't say no or refuse, as she didn't know what he might do, but the thought of his capabilities was enough for her to obey simply. Besides the chores and game shop, she had made friends rather than acquaintances in the street where they had moved in. Still, they were into all these things that terrified her, and they weren't precisely mature, like boys, alcohol, smoking, sex, violence, and all that. At the same time, she couldn't trust them about anything. I mean, she couldn't even be honest with herself. She hated herself for it, and her self-esteem couldn't have been any lower, or so she thought.

I mean, even the so-called "friends" she made her a push, which wasn't difficult as she had always been a people pleaser. Every time they visited her, the fridge was almost complete. Hence, they fry meat and take out anything edible, only for Victoria to return unexpectedly before she had even begun cleaning. They would scream, "Here's your mum", and when she turned, they were gone by the time Victoria reached the gate, and she was already yelling, "For your sake and mine, I hope you've cleaned my house."

She couldn't even respond. Victoria would ask, "What's that smell?" as she opened the fridge. "What on earth? There wasn't this much food in the fridge and cupboards when I left. What on earth did you do?"
    Zazi: uhm… nothing
    Victoria: Nothing you say? Why is that? When there are more dirty and greasy plates than I left, the frying pan is a mess, and it smells and looks like a pigsty in here.
    Zazi: I'm sorry …I…I…

Victoria: What? Has the cat got your tongue? Did I not give clear instructions when I left this morning?

As she closed the door and grabbed the broom behind it

Zazi: you did

Victoria: so why is my house a mess?

Zazi: I … I…I …I was …going to clean I promise

Victoria: So, what happened next? Did you choose to act like a big spender and give all our food to your mates?

Zazi: no…I…I

She slapped her repeatedly across the face, and as she fell to the floor, the broom struck her in the stomach, caught by Victoria's foot, which kicked her as she cried silently.

"Don't disrespect me in my home; this isn't your grandfather's place. Now, get up and tidy this house."

Zazi was still weeping when she bit her head off on some. "Quit crying and do as you are told; where's my child? Has she eaten? Or were you too busy feeding the whole neighbourhood to be bothered?

Zazi: I don't know

She grabbed the broom and struck Zazi's face without realising. She pummelled her mercilessly, again and again, saying, "Go find her before I sort you out." So she staggered out, barely walking correctly, and searched the park. She was with Byron and his friends, so she approached him and said, "Your aunt wants me to bring her daughter."

Byron: Are you referring to your sister?

Zazi: I don't have time. I need to take her home and do as I was instructed.

Byron: Alright, inform her that she's with me.

Zazi: well, she needs to have something to eat.

Byron: Right, cook and bring us some food.

She was so done with this that she rolled her eyes and walked away. Then she grabbed her, pulled her back, and said, "Don't you dare roll your eyes at me. She's your sister, which means she's your responsibility. You're lucky

I'm not reporting you, so BRING THE FOOD!"

Terrified to her core, she gently pulls her hand back and walks away, heading home to deliver the message to Victoria and inform her, "Zara is with Byron."
Victoria: has she eaten?
Zazi: I'm not sure. I didn't ask, so why not inquire with him?

She began cleaning, starting with the dishes, as instructed, so she could prepare some food for Victoria, as requested, and served her, "This tea is cold; I need it boiling." Zazi rushed to the kitchen to remake it, although she couldn't understand why, as the tea was steaming hot. At least she continued with her chores.
After she was done, she played games on Victoria's phone
"Zazi! Zazi!!! ZAZI!!!"
As she jolted awake, a little frightened, she thought, "Urgh! What have I done now?"
She answered, "Yes."
"I've been calling your name. What's wrong with you? Are you deaf?"
"I was asleep; why?"
Victoria: where's my phone?
Zazi:" It's on your bed."
Victoria: Where can I find it here?
She simply got up and fetched it, as this might have escalated into an unnecessary argument since she was attempting to return to her sleep. Yet again, she was screaming, "ZAZI!!"
Zazi: yes?!
Victoria: What did you do to my phone?
Zazi: nothing
Victoria: Don't bloody lie to me. You had my phone, and now it won't send or receive calls or messages.
Zazi: I don't know. I was just playing games
Victoria: you better tell me what you did to my phone
Before she could even speak, she hurled a mug at his face and shouted,

"Pick that bloody mug up and bring it here, then tell me what you did to my phone."

Zazi: nothing

Victoria: Well, fix it!

She threw the mug at her again, and before she could blink, the same phone flew in straight in her face and between her eyes. Victoria got up in a hurry, closed the door and pinned Zazi between the door and wall as she started hitting her with shoes and punches, almost landing her on a nail with her left eye whilst grabbing her leg, not giving her the slightest chance to breathe biting her with her teeth deep in her skin like she was trying to peel it off as Zazi screamed: "you are biting me."

She said, "Shut up and get out of my face, sending her running while quietly sobbing.

Yelling, "Don't you dare make a noise! Get up, make me some tea, and stop crying." She thought that if she acted as though she couldn't hear her, she would realise she was wrong. Instead, she yelled, "Do you want me to come over there and beat the muteness out of you?"

"No," she murmured. She got up, made herself some tea, and served it to her. After that, she returned to try and catch some sleep, hoping she wouldn't wake up with a swollen face. She still had school the following day and wasn't keen on answering questions about her bruises.

After a while, Victoria strolled into the lounge, radiating sunshine and rainbows, and remarked, "It seems the network was preventing me from sending texts, making calls, or even receiving any; my apologies!

What has happened to apologies and admitting one's faults? Or perhaps that only occurs in fairy tales. So Zazi didn't respond. Instead, she shut her eyes, attempting to sleep, but she couldn't help but weep…

Three

Fragile Connections

"Friendship can serve as a sanctuary, yet even safe havens have their shadows."

"At times, the safest places are not constructed with walls, but rather formed by the embrace of those who genuinely see you."

The next day, Victoria woke Zazi up for school. She had a bath and got dressed. Victoria seemed to have something to say, but unless it was an apology, Zazi couldn't be bothered. Therefore, she politely declined, claiming she had to rush to school as she stepped out. At school, she had an interesting group of friends with whom she walked to and from school. Their meeting spot was by the chicken farm, and as Zazi was heading straight past, she was met by Chelsea, who greeted her…

Zazi: Hey!

Chelsea: Morning, how are you?

Zazi: I'm OK, thanks. Are you? By the way, where's Kholofelo?

Chelsea: she's not coming to School today; she's sick and has to go to the doctor

Zazi: oh, I guess it's just the two of us, then

Chelsea: Well, let us commence with our walking, shall we?
She laughed and replied, "Let's!"

Zazi's two friends possessed an incredible ability to make her feel whole. They transformed her into a different, more vibrant person who didn't carry the world's weight. With them, she could be a child again, forgetting all her problems until the last period when the bell rang. After twenty minutes, they arrived at school, which wasn't far, and headed straight to the kitchen. Although Zazi wasn't usually one for breakfast, there was something about the way the aunties at school made porridge that had an alluring aroma, not to mention the addictive taste; thus, she couldn't miss it, despite the always-present queue in the kitchen, as she wasn't the only one who loved the porridge. She always made it her mission to arrive at school as early as possible to ensure she didn't miss out. Finally reaching the front of the line, the auntie greeted her with a big smile, saying, "Salaam Alaikum," as she handed Zazi her silver plate of porridge. "Walaykum salaam, auntie, and shukran!" Zazi replied, smiling back and receiving the plate with both hands. She had never imagined in her wildest dreams that she would speak Arabic, let alone be in a Muslim-dominated school that transformed into a mosque every day. After school, she recalled her first day at Talfalah. It had felt very uneasy for her as she struggled to pronounce certain words; she never understood why. When she blurted out "yeses," suddenly the whole class turned around and began chanting, "We are going to report you." She was confused. "Report me? Why?"

"You are swearing!!"

"Swearing? What is that I said that's swearing?"

"Well, we can't say it; it's a swear word."

"I just said yeses; what's vulgar about it?"

"You did it again."

At this point, Zazi's heart was racing. She had never liked trouble and was terrified of being in it, so she tried to ask what the word might mean. She wasn't one to swear, as she had been brought up better than her grandmother.

Shents had taught her well, but no one could answer her, so she decided to let it go.

However, who knew she would ultimately be happy at school and get along with everyone as if nothing had ever happened? School was her sanctuary. After a while, she returned to reality and remembered that she was eating, and her porridge was getting cold; she ate and made her way to class. Upon entering, she saw Azania (Aza), Ishmael, Brandon, and Hashim, her classmates whom she adored. Azania was a friend despite having dreadlocks and the most genuine smile she had ever seen. At times, she felt a pang of jealousy at how perpetually happy Azania always seemed, never sporting a frown or sad face, just forever cheerful; she wished she could experience that level of happiness, even if just once. Then there was Ishmael. He was charming and always had his hair hanging just above his eyes. A well-mannered boy, he enjoyed laughing and telling jokes, making him fun to be around. Next was Hashim, the tallest boy in the class. Following him was Brandon, probably the shortest boy in their year but also the cutest in Zazi's eyes. Of course, Brandon could be the sweetest while, at times, the meanest; he was always fooling around, especially if he didn't like someone, but he was consistently lovely to Zazi. Everyone was, and it seemed they could sense her pain and burdens, so she tried to lighten them. Regardless, Zazi was always grateful, as she had never been welcomed with such warmth when she arrived in Cape Town. She settled down as they waited for the rest of their class to come and for the bell to ring so that assembly could commence well outside their classrooms. Naturally, the entire school stood in line. Meanwhile, some students were busy trying to complete their homework.

Zazi never really understood how a person could have the entire weekend or day to complete their school work but still choose not to, opting to rush in late on Monday morning, indifferent to whether their work was right or wrong. Sihle and Keenan, Zazi's friends, were quite the troublemakers. Zazi found it impossible to accomplish anything with these two around; the boys enjoyed playing, but then again, they say, "Boys will be boys." As time passed, Zazi realised she was seated in the wrong crowd at the back of the classroom, surrounded by lads who never did their work, either too lazy or unwilling. She worried that they might drag her into trouble or tarnish her reputation, much like the one they had created for themselves. Still, everyone knew she was forever quiet and timid, and if she ever acted otherwise, these boys would be to blame for influencing the sweet, innocent, hard-working, and intelligent girl she was. The first period began. The class teacher was a handsome man in his early thirties, new to the school, and quite muscular; his wife was slender. Unlike most teachers, when he arrived, he never hit girls. He was a gentleman, only ever punishing the boys.

Mr Griever was undoubtedly the best teacher in Zazi's eyes. She had never encountered a man of his stature or calibre. At the same time, she could not understand why he chose to teach at Talfalah. Nevertheless, whatever the circumstances, she was grateful and always eager for his class. However, her classmates could never keep quiet or settle down, so he asked Aza to write down the names of the noisy students. She complied; he took a stick from the drums and struck everyone on that list, stating: "I don't believe in hitting or punishing learners, but I've been told it's the only way you know how to listen, and by the looks of it, I guess it's true."

Zazi was, to say the least, impressed. Students often walked all over him since he was new and didn't believe in physical punishment or discipline. However, he needed to set them straight, and surprisingly, they suddenly knew how to listen, complete their homework, and submit assignments and projects on time. Everything was going well until rumours began to circulate about Mr Griever having an affair at the school; apparently, he was a paedophile.

Zazi could not believe her ears. They had to be lying. No one seemed to like Mr Griever, not even the teachers, as he always sat by himself in his class, if not in the car park smoking; no one at school ever spoke to him apart from the students. When the rumours surfaced, he suddenly became so stressed that he was an entirely different person, constantly agitated and quick to anger; it was always clear that he had anger management issues, although who wouldn't be angry? What if his wife heard the news, or she had because she no longer drove him to school? He came on his bike or in his black private car.

Zazi felt sorry for him and wished she could help. She had a soft spot and thought, "If only they knew him like I did or saw him as I did." Her thoughts were of plain innocence, which she shouldn't have had, but he was always so kind and gentle that she couldn't see past his kindness, even when he was vulgar, which he argued was a slip of the tongue. The rumours, however, were escalating; he was no longer just a paedophile preying on his students. He was now said to be dating his colleague, so since the paedophilia accusations hadn't worked out as expected, this pathetic gossiper decided to change the narrative, regardless of the consequences it would have on the teacher's life.

The day was almost over, following a PE lesson after the second interval, which Zazi dreaded as she was never particularly active. There were numerous sports, such as volleyball, shot put, and running, and the losses continued. She couldn't even decline, as it was compulsory according to the school syllabus.

Not volleyball, pool, or even football. For the most part, she had the opportunity to learn a new language, Afrikaans, which she didn't know—not even how to greet in it. This was somewhat challenging, yet she still passed with flying colours, which was impressive given that it was foreign to her. The school was the right place for Zazi. She wasn't participating in PE, but she sometimes had fun. She just never liked to sweat, having done enough of that at home, juggling school and her sister, which was tough for a twelve-year-old while dealing with the boys in the neighbourhood, including Byron. Still, she had to soldier on, and as Tupac Shakur said: "Baby, don't cry, keep your head baby, don't cry…"

Four

Price of Escape

"*Leaving doesn't erase the pain, but sometimes, it offers a chance to breathe again.*"

"*Escape is not freedom, but it is the first step toward reclaiming the life stolen from you.*"

The school day had ended. Zazi had to get home, which she dreaded, but she arrived eventually; she undressed and put on something more comfortable than her school uniform. She passed Victoria's preschool, spotted her sister, and immediately kept walking. She would have stayed with her sister but felt compelled to be elsewhere as she marched to the game shop, regretting the day she was born, knowing Dwayne wouldn't leave her alone. On this particular day, she felt she lacked the strength to fight him, though things were different this time since Zazi was caught with Dwayne. The sad part is that the boy who saw them didn't understand what was happening; from his perspective, she was a whore as he looked at her while standing by the half-closed door. After Dwayne realised someone was watching, he quickly got up, pulled up his pants, and zipped them, fastening his belt while the boy hid. "Get up, pull up your pants, wait at least five minutes until I've left, then leave too," he commanded as he ran out.

Boy: Can I also tap that? I promise I won't tell a soul.

That was the least shocking thing Zazi had heard from a bloke, and she couldn't feel any dirtier or more disgusted with herself, so she simply fled without saying a word. The closer she got to home, the more she noticed Byron's mates. They had been waiting for her, standing there and blocking the street.

"Here we go again," she thought as her instinct screamed, "Cover your face she pulled the laces of her hoodie up, but it was too late. They had already seen her "whore!" they changed "slut" they continued the way they were dishing out insults it was as if they read them off a book. She wanted to run but felt too overwhelmed by the attention. At the same time, she didn't want others to think she was a whore because she wasn't—or was she? She couldn't decide. All she knew was that whatever their claims were, they didn't matter. What would she have said? No one would believe that she was forced, overpowered, held against her will, or threatened. Better yet, they wouldn't understand. She eventually got home with all that. As she walked in, Victoria was there, shocking her. "Your grandmother called," she said.

Zazi: What? Why?

She was so excited that she couldn't even conceal it.

Victoria: She says that your grandfather is alone during the week, and she doesn't like that, so she wants you to go back

Zazi: well, yes, of course! What did you say to her?

Victoria: Well, I said no, of course, wasn't sure, and told her to call again

Zazi: why would you do that? Call her and tell her I want to go back …

Of course, she did. She would have been damned if she had stayed here a minute longer.

Victoria: Call her yourself

Before she could even reach for the phone, it rang. Speak of the devil, as she answered.

Zazi: hello?

Granny: greetings, child; how are you?

Zazi: I'm great, thanks, and you?

Granny: I'm a delicate child! Good to hear from you. Could you please come back? Your grandfather is all alone here as everyone has graduated, and I work out of town, only returning on the weekends.

Zazi: oh, say no more gladly; I would be thrilled to come back

Granny: great! Well, we will require your report transfer letter from the school you are at so we can find you another school here

Zazi: yes, of course

Her excitement was uncontrollable as her grandmother said, "Okay, let me talk to your mother." She handed the phone over.

They spoke on the phone for a while, and Victoria kept responding with "yes" and nothing more. Zazi, curious about what was being asked or stated, grew so severe that she continued to answer like a substitute, obeying her master or taking orders.

Finally, she hung up, and she didn't look too happy. Zazi would have thought she would be glad to be rid of her at last, but then again, she might miss having her punching bag. Zazi couldn't stand her gawking in absolute silence, so she blurted out, "What is it?"

Victoria: Do you wish to leave?

Zazi: yes!

Victoria: you didn't even consider it, yet you simply agreed.

Zazi: There wasn't anything to think about

Victoria: Do you really hate me that much?

At this stage, Zazi was so fed up with this conversation that she never wanted to be there. She hardly spoke, let alone converse. She had given reasons, and besides, she had left her father first. Her behaviour of acting like a victim just seemed pitiful.

Zazi: I hate it here, plus I thought you said granny kicked me out

Victoria: well, she did

Zazi: why? I mean, I never did anything.

Victoria: I have no idea. It's about that saga between you, me, and your aunt during your great-grandmother's funeral.

Zazi: right!

Zazi nodded, reluctant to probe further because she knew Victoria would lie regardless. She never believed anything Victoria said; in this instance, Victoria had never taken the time to earn that level of respect or trust. She had merely waltzed into Zazi's life and wreaked havoc without a care in the world. Zazi was counting the moments until she could return home, escape this mess, and avoid Dwayne, Byron, and his friends altogether.

Zazi felt overwhelmed, pondering how she would embrace her granddad when she looked at him. She missed him deeply and realised that if her mother hadn't forced her to come along, she would never have experienced any of the moments she shared with her; regardless of everything, she craved that hug. She longed to let it all out on his shoulder. After all, her grandfather was the only father figure she had known, and she simply needed her father—both of her parents, actually, her grandparents. At the same time, she was furious with them; why had they allowed Victoria to take her? Why? Why?

The school year had already ended. Zazi had finished her work. All that was left was to fetch her report, although Victoria could do that. Then, finally, she could go! She had been waiting for this day for far too long. If there truly is a God, her silent cries have never fallen on deaf ears.

Later that day, Victoria took Zazi and Zara to a place known only to her, with several women, many of whom were older, at least in Zazi and Zara's eyes. The house was filled with numerous women and items like animal skins. Some women there sported beads, including Sangomas (traditional healers). The floor was strewn with alcohol—brandy, beer, wine, and various types of each; some of the women were tipsy, some were drunk, and one or two lay passed out on the grass mat on the floor.

Victoria greeted: hello.

The women: sit down

So we sat, and as soon as we did, a couple of shots were passed around, including a couple for me, so I just held one and looked at Victoria.

"Oh well, don't look at me, drink," she said

Without hesitation, Zazi downed a shot of brandy, leaving an immediate burn in her throat. The drink was bitter, pungent, and hot, the heat coursing through her taste buds so intensely that she couldn't maintain a straight face. Despite it not being her first encounter with brandy, she still struggled to avoid twitching or contorting her expression. The drinks continued to be passed around, though Victoria began to feel a bit concerned as she remarked.

"Zazi, please drink one thing at a time. Don't mix wine and beer with brandy; stick to the brandy."

Zazi: okay

So she did as she was told. She never wanted to drink wine or beer; it wasn't her cup of tea, even though she shouldn't have been drinking alcohol at all. After all, she was just twelve years old. The drinks kept coming at a relentless pace. Zazi didn't realise how much she had consumed until her head began to feel a bit heavy. At first, she felt slightly dizzy, so she decided to stay put, not wanting anyone to notice. Although one of the ladies was oblivious, she asked, "Are you still alive over there?"

Zazi: as fresh as a daisy

Victoria: No, you're drunk.

Zazi: not in the slightest. I …

Victoria: Right, stand up and take a few steps. Let's see how you go.

Zazi didn't like being daring, so she got up with her body feeling so heavy it felt like gravity was pulling her, leaving her with no control over her movements. Still, she wasn't about to let her temper get the better of her. Thus, she decided to make her way to the toilet. She needed to pee; her feet were staggering as soon as she stepped outside. The grass seemed to hold her back, and the breeze slapped her cheeks so forcefully that she nearly sobered up before returning inside to sit down, reaching for yet another glass.

On the other hand, Victoria decided it was enough, as she wasn't in the mood to carry anyone or deal with trouble, and perhaps she shouldn't have let her drink in the first place. Meanwhile, Zazi sat there with her head between her knees, utterly bored as she tried to keep up with the cheddar. Still, it started to get rather hot, and she needed some air. This time, when she stepped out of the door, she tripped. "Oops! Clumsy me," she thought… so she simply sat there until her backside became sore. She decided to get up, but it was a bit tricky. Still, she got up, eventually, fumbling her walk into the toilet, pulled her pants down and her behind along with as her buttocks landed on the toilet seat so hard she almost didn't make it up, not to mention she nearly wet herself instead, her body became heavier. Consequently, she remained seated for a time as she collected her strength to recover. Ultimately, after almost losing consciousness in the toilet, she resolved to stand up. One might expect Brandy to burn off some calories rather than gain more weight. She pulled up her trousers, but she forgot her knickers at her knees. Now she had to bend down and retrieve her knickers and these very tight jeans. Thus, as she bent down with her head feeling so heavy, she could see and feel the ground beneath her spinning, almost touching the concrete floor and breaking into the cement in the bathroom. She tried her best to get up while balancing her hands on the wall quickly, but they were all sweaty and slippery. Consequently, she had to lift her head from her knees and support herself with her head against the wall, pulling down both her panties and jeans as she rose, zipped up her jeans, and staggered outside as her feet slipped. She tripped. Fortunately, she didn't fall. She managed to balance as she gradually brought her feet and legs together, attempting to lift each leg slowly and carefully. As she headed towards the door, she froze, struggling not to collapse onto the floor as Victoria remarked, "Oh well, somebody's drunk."

Zazi: I'm not drunk

Victoria: It's not a crime; you can admit it.

Though it was her age regardless, she remained quiet, stepped outside, and sat down. She dozed off and heard a voice say, "Let's go home."

As Victoria waved goodbye to her friends, Zazi struggled to stand up straight. Victoria put her arm around Zazi's shoulder, assisting her as she stumbled and fell. Victoria then had to lift her. Although Zazi couldn't comprehend much, neither of them could make sense of the situation as Zazi had stopped drinking hours earlier; thus, she shouldn't have become intoxicated. They managed to get a taxi, which was the last thing Zazi remembered before everything went dark for her...

Five

A New Kind of Hurt

"The weight of trauma lingers, weaving itself into moments that should be light."

"The weight of pain may bend you, but it is the decision to rise that determines if it will break you."

Days later, after that night when Zazi got drunk, much was left blurred for her as she struggled to remember.

However, who could blame her? It was a festive season, a time for celebrations, not that there was much for her to celebrate. She and her friends had pooled money to do something fun, so they bought some steak and a few goodies. Zazi, however, left them to get some liquor, as they weren't in the mood for alcohol today of all days, which Zazi found ironic. Anyway, she left, heading to another street in the neighbourhood to Steve's House, where they sell beverages; it was a local tavern. She bought herself a drink, took a few sips, and was soon drunk. The next thing she knew, Byron's friends were walking towards her, one of whom was the guy Zack she had been forced to date. He seemed reluctant to walk as his friends dragged him along. On the other hand, Zazi happened to trip and landed on his lips as he recoiled, wiping his mouth and spitting. After that, she felt embarrassed and tried to walk away, but Akhona wouldn't let them leave each other's sight, forcing Zack to kiss and hug her. She kept losing her balance as they laughed, and as she walked home, she felt humiliated, barely able to walk. When she got home, she swung the door open to find Victoria in shock. "And then?" Zazi was taken aback as she tried to steady herself, seeing that her mum had company.

"Zazi, are you drunk?"

Zazi couldn't fathom why people would notice you were out of it and still ask.

Zazi: No, ma'am.

Victoria: Are you sure? Stand on one leg.

She stood on one leg so perfectly that, if it hadn't been so evident she was indeed intoxicated, she might have believed herself. However, she wasn't trying to hide it as she staggered her way to the kitchens, grabbing whatever she could find from the pots on the stove and shoving it into her mouth so fast and impatiently that she didn't even wait to swallow after entering the room, trying to sleep but unable to do so.

She heard voices in the lounge. It was Victoria and another familiar voice, so she investigated the commotion.

"Oh! Zazi, thank goodness I found you. I'm trying to locate Azola; I can't seem to find her."

Zazi: Oh! The last time I saw her was in the afternoon before I left them at Yammy's place.

Azola's mum: Well, I went there, and they don't know where she is, and she's drunk.

This was news to Zazi, for when she left the group, they didn't seem particularly keen to drink any alcohol. She stormed off in search of her right after she turned the corner and passed through a shady passage; there she was. Zazi did her utmost to convince a drunk and aggressive Azola to come home but to no avail. So, she returned home to inform her mum that she had found her, but she wouldn't come along; instead, she was being violent, throwing bricks at her.

Azola's mum: I'm sorry to hear that. Please keep an eye on her and make sure she's safe.

So Zazi went back again and, this time, found her wandering about as if she were searching for something; she stopped every single man she saw who was climbing and tried to strip them naked. Zazi did her utmost to stop her. "Azola, stop! What are you doing?' She wouldn't answer or hear her. She appeared possessed; instead of stopping her actions, she continued throwing bricks at Azola. Although Azola was also drunk, she had sobered up due to the situation and felt confused and terrified, unsure of what to do or say. She remembered her mother advising her to take care of her, but how can one care for someone who is trying to harm them? As Azola led her on a wild goose chase, this was. Not to mention the judgemental stares from bystanders, especially towards Zazi, who was not even attempting to help. At the same time, Azola managed to pin another man against a wall or, rather, the man allowed it, removing his boxers. The man wasn't even trying to stop her. He was sober, even complaining, "You're going to get arrested," although Zazi couldn't see through the smirk on his face.

Zazi: push her off

The man: I can't. She's too strong.

How ironic that an 11-year-old, skinny and tiny girl was too strong for a man in his forties; that was the most ridiculous thing. Zazi wished he could have simply admitted he was enjoying the ride. Zazi hated every minute of this but couldn't do anything about it, yet she still couldn't leave because she was supposed to protect her friend. But how was she supposed to do that when she was merely a child, standing there in utter shock, unable to believe she was screaming at the man, "Do something!!!"

Man: No, you do something. She's your friend.

Zazi: I'm trying, but as you can see, she's attacking me, and you're the adult here.

At that point, she simply wanted to beat some sense into Azola, but she knew she didn't stand a chance, and with Azola, fights are never-ending. Azola jumped around this man, and Zazi felt powerless and lost, unsure of what to do, and she couldn't bear to watch all of this. She left, considering whether to tell Azola's mum, but what could she say? There were no right words or phrases to form to convey such news to a parent about her 11-year-old... As she entered the gate, she saw Azola's mum leaving but couldn't even bring herself to look at her. She hurried inside before she could ask anything, trying to locate Victoria. As she continued to think about how she ought to look after her friend instead, she accompanied and walked her through a slaughterhouse.

Victoria: What's the matter? Why are you crying?
Zazi : iiiii…iiiii …it's Azola
Victoria: what about her?
Zazi: she's… she's…
Victoria: speak child!!
Zazi: you need to see for yourself
Victoria: just tell me
Zazi: Azola is drunk, out of control, and she's… She's uhm
Victoria: she's what?
Zazi: striping men naked and climbing them
Victoria: why didn't you tell her mother?
Zazi: and say what?
Victoria: What did you just say? Wait, you didn't.
Zazi: No!
Victoria: why didn't you stop her?
Zazi: excuse me? I tried, but she was hitting and throwing bricks at me
Victoria: so where is she now?
Zazi left her with that man.
Victoria: who's this man?

Zazi felt irritated because she couldn't comprehend why Victoria overwhelmed her with so many questions instead of speaking to Azola's mother or attempting to assist Azola herself.

Zazi: Do you know him? He has a lump-like protrusion on his cheek; he's light-skinned and bald-headed.

Victoria: I don't know him

Zazi: well, if you were to come with me, you might get to know him.

Victoria: Come where? I'm not going anywhere

Zazi: so what am I to do? Leave her there?

Victoria: I don't know. Tell her mother

Zazi: I can't, which is why I told you instead, so you would either do something or inform her.

Victoria: well, it's neither my problem nor yours.

Zazi: heh! Gee! Thanks for your help

Zazi dashed outside, returning to where she had last seen Azola, hoping she would still be there—ideally not in the same situation, but she was; she failed once more to get the man to stop. They simply continued while people passed by, doing nothing but exchanging nasty remarks and judgemental glances. Instead, she went to Azola's place and fetched her mother. She couldn't bring herself to tell her what was happening with her daughter, so she showed her instead. She dreaded seeing her reaction, so she went home. After hours of tossing and turning in her bed, she still felt terrible, worried, and stressed about what had transpired. Eventually, she drifted off to sleep. Her head spun so much that she couldn't keep her eyes open. Thank goodness she was in bed at the time. It felt like she had just blinked, and it was already the next day as Victoria woke her up, saying, "Get up."

"No, just a few more minutes", Zazi muttered

Victoria: No, I can manage that. You are leaving today, remember?

Zazi: I am? Where to?

Victoria: Queenstown

Zazi: but I've barely even slept

Victoria: well, your transport gets here at 5 am, so chop, chop!

Zazi: why so early?

Victoria: perhaps it's because Queenstown is quite far, and they aim to leave Cape Town by 8 am

Zazi hated being woken up, especially having her sleep interrupted, so even though she wanted to leave, she preferred departing while still asleep. Even if she wasn't seen, she detested having to wake up this early … It wouldn't be,

Zazi: can't I go another day?

Victoria: nope, you wanted to leave, right?

Zazi: It's not that I don't want to leave; I just need to sleep for a few minutes.

Victoria: no! You'll sleep in the car.

As Zazi was particularly reluctant and took ages to get out of bed, Victoria had no choice but to undress, bathe herself, and get dressed alongside her sister, Zara. She needed to be quick, as their transport would arrive any minute.

"Take your bags outside."

As the car flashed its lights and started honking outside, "Yay!" Zazi felt excited, knowing it was time to go home, yet she wished she could already be there. The driver ran around Cape Town briefly as Zazi gazed out the window, watching the sky clear and the sun grow brighter and hotter. She tapped her foot impatiently beneath the seat; it was 8 am, and they should have been out of Cape Town by now. Just when she thought they were about to leave, they had to switch taxis, as the current one was a bit too cramped for the number of passengers on this trip. After all the stops, they were finally out of Cape Town and headed to Queenstown. Although the journey was exhausting, she had expected her sister to give her trouble in the car, but Zara was as quiet as a graveyard. The taxi stopped after a few hours of driving, mainly to fill up on diesel and allow people to relieve themselves so they could use the bathrooms in the garages or buy food. On one occasion, Zazi decided to step into the garage, thinking her sister might need to use the toilet or fancy some snacks. Inside the shop, Zara insisted on getting her snacks and refused to share, wanting to buy out the entire store while Zazi tried to politely decline her requests, explaining that there wasn't enough money to buy all of those things. The little rascal wouldn't hear of it; she pushed the shelf, causing bags of crisps and other items to tumble. Zara threw the biggest tantrum, making a scene by crying, yelling, and throwing things about. Zazi noticed that everyone in the shop looked at her, which she found pretty uncomfortable. Embarrassed and angry, Zazi wasn't going to give in. She went to the till, paid, and left Zara, her four-year-old sister, at the shop, thinking, "When she's done with all her whining, she can follow. Otherwise, I'll leave her here." After a while, Zara must have realised that her sister was no longer in the shop, as she soon followed suit when the people in the taxi asked, "Where's the child?"

"At the store"

"What do you mean at the store?"

"I left her there."

"Why? That child is very young; what if she gets lost?"

"Then minus one problem for me

"Go and get the child.'

"I'm sure she can find her way."

"Don't be stubborn"

"If anything, she's the stubborn one, and Frankly, I don't mind leaving her here."

Zazi's replies animated the mother in the taxi, but she still wouldn't budge. Zazi couldn't care less, so she allowed them to ramble on; one lady wanted to fetch Zara, but she was already there, and the driver got her inside. She came and sat quietly beside Zazi. Her soft face was all pink, and her eyes were red from crying. It had Zazi chuckling, and she couldn't help but laugh. Zazi brought out some biscuits and the lunch box her mum had packed and handed them to her to eat. Noticing the dryness of her lips, it was clear she was starving. "Is everyone inside?" the driver inquired. "Yes," the passengers replied. They swung the door shut, got in, and were back on the road again. So the entire journey consisted of driving, stopping, going to the toilet, eating, sleeping, waking up and doing it all over again, while their grandparents kept calling every 30 minutes to check on their safety or if they were still travelling well and praying for them. In contrast, their mother went silent—no texts, no calls, just pure silence.

They finally reached Queenstown, and their grandfather came to fetch them at the engine garage; Zazi was so exhausted from the journey that she passed out in the car. They were finally home after a long drive; Zazi looked at the yard and felt as though it was unreal. It seemed like aeons since she had last set foot in her home. It was almost too good to be true. Grandad helped them with the luggage; Zazi was quite pleased with her sister's quietness before anything else. Zazi had to search the whole house for her grandmother. She leaned in and felt herself melt like ice on a hot stove when she saw her. The greeting was brief, and then Zazi rushed to her room to get some sleep. It had been a long ride. She was woken by the loud peals of laughter echoing in the hallway. She could have sworn Trevor Noah must have been entertaining them, only to make her way to where everyone was seated and see her sister holding down the fort, and she couldn't be more annoyed.

"Zazi!" Her grandmother yelled

Zazi: yes, grams?

Grandma: Your food is in the microwave. You must be starving, and there's juice in the fridge.

Zazi: thanks, grandma. Indeed I am

She went to the fridge for some juice and then ate. Her grandfather gazed at her so intensely that it felt like he could see right through her.

Grandpa: Zazi!

Zazi: yes, grandpa?

Grandpa: are you ok?

Zazi: yeah, why do you ask?

Grandpa: you just look a little off for my liking

Zazi: OH, I never knew you had a liking

Grandpa: well, you've been quiet ever since you got here, and it's not like you at all

Zazi: I'm fine, Grandpa. I'm just tired.

If only Mr Richards knew that Zazi was no longer the little girl he had raised, the sunshine that radiated through her eyes would have faded, leaving only coldness and her pale skin. It wasn't just Zazi who had changed; her aunt Tamara had had a baby. Oh, she certainly knew how to make haste with that one. Zazi spent most of the holidays in Lady Frere, where Victoria eventually joined her and Zara. Zazi had missed the scent of the wet red soil – ah! Indeed, there's no place like home – as she inhaled…

Six

Carrying the Weight

"Strength is the quiet determination to continue pressing on, even when the road seems endless."

"There is strength in survival, even when the heart feels unbearably heavy to bear."

January arrived, signalling a return to school; Victoria and Zara were back in Cape Town, and Zara couldn't be happier that things were returning to normal. In her home, Cape Town, she felt, as she had during the holidays, that her sister was stealing her spotlight, as her grandparents seemed to have forgotten about her and were instead fawning over Zara. "Hush! Zazi, jealousy is a disease," she admonished herself, inhaling and exhaling as she attempted to calm down. With school about to resume and Zazi starting at a new school, she and her granddad went shopping at Strauss for her school uniform; upon arrival, they greeted a lady who came by with, "Yes, sir! How may I assist you?"

Grandpa: Yes, young lady, I am searching for a school dress for this thing behind me.

Zazi couldn't believe her ears. "This thing," he said as the lady pointed behind her. "This way!"

She chose a school dress and said, "Here, try it on." The dress appeared enormous. She wanted to go to a fitting room, but her grandpa insisted she remain and measure it by laying it against her chest.

"That's not your size. I'll get another one," the kind lady said
"Don't bother; this one is fine", the grandfather said
Zazi: Grandpa, this is way too big
Grandpa: looks decent to me
Zazi couldn't shake the feeling that she shouldn't have come and that her grandad should have done the shopping instead of what he was doing now.
"Well, it does look quite big; there is one that might fit, let me…"
Grandpa: Don't worry, we're fine. All we need is a green school jacket (raincoat) jacket.

As she cut her off literally, the poor lady rushed to the side of the jackets and showed Mr Richards that it was as if this were his uniform, and Zazi thought it best to let him do his thing. After all, he is an adult, so he knows better. "Try this one on. Let's see if it fits," the lady said as Zazi snapped out of her thoughts. She took it and tried it on, and although it was huge once more before she could say anything, he exclaimed, "Perfect!" even though the arms of the jacket hung down like long wires.

"Anything else?" The lady asked
Grandpa: no thanks
Lady: what about a jersey and pants or a school blazer?
Grandpa: a blazer we can take for the rest; we will be fine
Lady: you barely bought much
Grandpa: with reason, so get me the blazer, will you? Thank you

As he crossed his arms and rested them on his thighs, bending his knees up and down, he seemed about to whistle, as usual. But no, this time, he simply tilted his head and stared through the ceiling as though he had X-ray vision.

The lady returned with the blazer. "This will cost R750

Grandpa: we will take it, Zazi grab it; let's go pay
Lady: Are you sure there's nothing else?
Grandpa: A hundred per cent now, if you'll excuse us, these won't pay themselves

As he walked towards the till, Zazi was amazed by how words simply jumped out of her grandpa; he never pondered his replies or questions. We stood in a queue, waiting for our turn to pay. Finally, they reached the till, paid, and were on their way. Once home, her grandad immediately ordered her to prepare something to eat, so she made a sandwich for both of them, brewed tea for her old man, and poured juice for herself; they both ate and chatted. Zazi could never express how much she missed those moments. There was also a new face in the house, and to Zazi's surprise, it was her little brother, a tiny creature her 18-year-old aunt now had as her bundle of joy. She should have seen him during the holidays, but she and her son had dashed off to Mount Fletcher for a while to her maternal home. The baby was light-skinned, had no hair, and was relatively small. He was only four months old when they named him Buhle, which meant beauty; indeed, he was beautiful. They had also hired a nanny for him. Her name was Sinoovuyo, but Zazi never called her by that name, just *sisi*. As much as this little bundle had brought joy to everyone, the one who brought him into the world didn't seem too pleased with herself or the baby. Zazi wanted to hold the baby, but her grandparents were concerned that she might drop him. "Don't get me wrong, I know I'm clumsy, but not that clumsy," she argued.

"We don't want to take any chances," they said

After eating, Zazi remembered that the following day was school, and before she could organise her uniform, she had to offload, so she darted off to the bathroom! "Za!!" She hated being disturbed while in the toilet, but it felt urgent. She pulled up her trousers and wondered what her grandma might want. "Yes, grandma?!"

Grandma: bring your uniform so I can iron it for you
Zazi: of course

Grandma: I'm unsure why you needed reminding; you know the routine.
Zazi: well, it's been a while, so you know...
Grandma: just bring me your uniform
Zazi: yes, ma'am!

She sped off in a flash to get her uniform: just five shirts, a navy school dress, a white and navy tracksuit, a navy school tie, five white socks, and a black school shoe that she had to polish herself. She took the shirts, school dress, tracksuit, and tie to her grandmother in the laundry room, placing them on the washing machine while her grandmother was still busy with her and her grandfather's outfits for work in the morning. After ironing everyone's clothes, her grandmother returned them to each room individually.

"Do these fit you?" She said, pointing to the school dress
Zazi: why do you ask?
Grandmother: I mean, you've grown but not enough to fit into these
Zazi: Your husband chose them for me, so I'm confident he knew what he was doing.
Grandmother: what were you doing?
Zazi: Trying not to get my head bitten off
Grandmother: well, good choice, then
She giggled, "Put these in a hangar somewhere, then polish your school shoes; it's school tomorrow."
Zazi: yes, grandmother!
Grandmother: are you ready?
Zazi: I don't have much of a choice in the matter
Grandmother: True that! Anyway, let me go and cook, and you get yourself ready.
Zazi: ok grandmother

As Sophie left her room to prepare her supper, Zazi took her school shoes (toughees) to the laundry, polished them, and then placed them near the washing machine, as she didn't want to dirty the mat in her room. She then returned to her room and was suddenly engulfed in deep thoughts. She must have zoned out for a bit, and time flew by; it was now "Time to pray", so she made her way to the living room. Upon entering, she found everyone already on their knees, so she, too, got down on hers without wasting time. For someone raised in this house, she had never truly believed, and sometimes, when they prayed together like this, it sounded more like a cult to her. She could never understand the unnecessary shouting and screaming as if "God" wouldn't hear them; indeed, they could pray more quietly. After the prayer, Zazi realised that Tamar and Buhle weren't there as she passed the door to her room. Buhle wouldn't stop crying and screaming; Tamara wasn't trying to calm him down. It was as if she wasn't even there, so angrily, Zazi swung the door open, was met with her fierce fireballs, and immediately apologised, saying, "Sorry, I thought he was alone."

Tamara: so? Who permitted you to get inside my room?

Zazi: Well, I just had to make sure, I'll leave now

Tamara: wait, you came for him, right?

Zazi: yes

Tamara: take him, he's giving me a headache. He won't bloody shut up

Zazi wasted no time in taking him into her arms

Zazi: Thanks

As soon as she picked him up and he fell into her arms, he remained quiet, prompting her to take him to her room.

"Oh, and if your grandparents ask, just say you offered to take him".

Zazi: of course

As much as Zazi was pleased that Buhle had settled down, she couldn't believe how tiny a creature he was; she couldn't fathom how anyone could have been that small at some point. So, she sat with him on the bed as he appeared rather sleepy.

"Zazi!!!"

"Coming?" she yelled back.

Grandma: Be careful! Your food is right there on the counter. You're not carrying my grandson while running like that, are you?

Zazi: Nope! I wasn't running; I was merely trying to arrive here in time without you thinking I was disregarding you.

Grandma: well, let me take him off your hands

Zazi: no, it's fine

Grandma: either way, how will you eat?

Zazi: I'll make do

Grandma: Hand him to me, eat, and then return to bed; it's an early morning, remember? New school and all that.

Zazi: right!

As she handed the baby to her grandmother.

Zazi ate, returned her bowl to the kitchen, and went to her room. She couldn't decide whether to be excited about tomorrow or anxious, but she couldn't shake off the feeling of nervousness. A knock on the door disturbed her as it was left ajar, hitting the table with the sewing machine behind it, and then she heard footsteps as she slowly opened her eyes, drifting away to the kitchen. She didn't even realise how or when she had fallen asleep and couldn't believe it was already morning, so she got up; it was time for a bath. She loved school but dreaded waking up early.

She finally bathed and dressed, fetched her shoes from the laundry room, proceeded to the bathroom to brush her teeth, and then returned to the kitchen. Her grandfather had made breakfast, and although she couldn't stomach food, she didn't want to seem rude, so she simply sat down and nibbled at her meal. They finished breakfast, and Zazi washed their bowls in the sink, dried them, and returned them to the cupboard. After this, she followed her grandfather to brush her teeth again, ensuring her teeth were clean before her grandpa noticed the mess she had made in the bathroom. She wiped the sink dry, then dashed outside to fetch the mop and attempted to mop the floor, but as the mop was wet, she resorted to using her foot to wipe the bathroom floor with several mats on the white tiles. Just then, she heard the gate open outside and knew it was time to leave. She hurried to her room, grabbed her backpack, and ran outside. Her grandfather was already waiting by the gate as she closed it one by one behind her. Eventually, she hopped into the car, and they set off. She was on her way to school, and her grandpa had to take her there, which wasn't even on his route to work, before finally heading to his job.

Zazi's grandfather, Mr. Richards, worked at the Department of Agriculture in Lady Frere. He was a farmer higher up the ranks, handling paperwork in the office. They arrived at Zazi's school, where her grandpa wished her luck on her first day before speeding off. As Zazi wandered around the school, mesmerised by the establishment, she noticed that the entire building, especially the classrooms, was made of wood. It was time for assembly as they stood and gathered in lines in front of their classrooms, just as they had done at Talfalah.

Right after the assembly, they were assigned to their registered classes. Zazi was now in the 6th grade, 6D to be precise. The first couple of periods passed; they weren't doing much since it felt like the first day. Timetables had to be prepared, books issued, and textbooks handed out. Hours went by, with the bell ringing repeatedly. It must have rung four times before the break; after another ring, they returned to their classes. The bell rang again, and finally, when it rang for the last time, the school was out.

It was time to go home. Zazi didn't know her way back, so she had to wait for her grandpa, regardless of when he finished work, which he never mentioned. She sat at the gate for a while, feeling as patched as she was and quite hungry. Fortunately, vendors outside the school gate sold everything from chips, vetkoeks, and buns to ice, chilled drinks, and fish. So, she bought the fish, hoping its oil would quench her thirst as she waited for her dear grandpa. After a while, there was suddenly no sign of anyone at the school. Finally, she saw the white Toyota Hilux swerve in front of her and stop at the corner as she rushed across the road. She opened the door, climbed in, and greeted, "Hey, Grandpa."

Grandpa: Greetings and apologies for keeping you waiting. I received assistance at work and thought I would arrive on time.

Zazi: it's fine

Grandpa: I need to arrange transport for you, as I'm worried you might get hurt waiting here all alone while I finish at 5 pm

Zazi: ok

Zazi was pleased she wouldn't have to wait, yet saddened that she wouldn't see her grandpa's face when driving home from school.

Seven

Cost of Betrayal

"*Trust is fragile, built slowly but shattered in an instant—yet we seek it still.*"

"*Betrayal doesn't destroy trust entirely; it simply teaches you who never deserved it.*"

The year had passed so quickly that Zazi was no longer a new student; she had made friends, in addition to the relentless homework, assignments, etc. Furthermore, Zazi frequently fell behind for various reasons, whether it was being late, allegedly making noise in class, or submitting incomplete homework, which was the norm with her Math teacher, Mrs Dada, and her English and Social Science teachers. Then there was the Afrikaans teacher, Mr Winner, who seemed lackadaisical in his duties as he rarely taught anything of substance. Instead, he would distribute tests and classwork but never assign homework, always providing the answers without checking whether his students could arrive at their own conclusions.

Mr Winner was an elderly man who spoke as if his lips ached and couldn't move, leaving anyone able to make sense of anything he said. Thus, whenever

Mr. Winner distributed tests, Zazi would begin writing her answers while he was still handing out the question papers to the rest of the class. She never liked cheating, and if she was to pass, she needed to do so on her terms. By the time Mr. Winner had finished, she would already be done.

Then there was Mr. Hartnick, who taught them Natural Sciences. For a chap over 70, he should have long since retired, yet he was as healthy as an ox and fresh as a daisy. Mr. Hartnick, being the best teacher and adored by the entire school, came with his troubles, as his name was always associated with scandalous rumours. First, it was said he had an affair with the janitor, Bongiwe, who, more than once, carried herself as if she owned the school and forced students to do her work. At the same time, she dipped her tongue down Mr Hartnick's throat, despite him being decades older than her. Then, the rumour had it that he was dating Mrs Dick, who was also younger and very much married – scandalous! It was no longer a shock but a formality as time passed.

Zazi had managed to make friends and acquaintances. One was a girl named Bridgette Sishuba, who shared a similar background with Zazi. Bridgette was very light-skinned; she nearly appeared white, had blond hair, and was a slim and beautiful, sweet child. Like Zazi, she never knew her father. Her mother was a wreck, and they didn't get along; her grandmother and uncle raised her. Despite being so sweet, she always seemed troubled. It seemed home wasn't as homely, as she was often bruised and pink, with maps all over her body, heavy eyes, and cheeks flushed red as if she hadn't slept a wink. She lived in a township called Nomzamo, and the kids at school mocked her as nobody knew what she was. A white girl may have been picked up in a dumpster by a black family. A coloured girl trying too hard to be white? Or just a white girl seeking approval, although they all called her an albino since she was too white to be black yet too black to be white.

Zazi never understood why the other kids couldn't simply let her be. Bridgette was the first girl Zazi befriended, as they were both seen as outcasts and quite a pair. Zazi had a whole group of friends outside it, like Thandolwethu (Thando) and Thandolwethu Lunda, who lived in Ezibeleni in the suburban area of Themba. Thando had a somewhat similar situation to Zazi, though it was quite the opposite for her. Thando was raised by her grandmother, her father's mother, who had never known her mother. Her mother fled as soon as she was born, leaving her at her father's doorstep, but she never returned. On the other hand, her father lived in Gauteng, and Thando rarely saw him as he had another family there. Thando preferred living with her grandmother over her father, and the supposed stepmother and her children made it all the more difficult for her to get closer to her dad.

Getting used to the once-upon-a-time new school also meant acclimatising to the fights that erupted occasionally. However, since violence was not Zazi's forte, she was regarded as a creep and a weirdo for refusing to watch, boo, or cheer. So whenever fights broke out, she would walk away, not wanting to hear the details the next day. She never fully understood what it was with people and violence, as it always seemed to be seen as the solution to everything, as though whatever happened to talking or working things out. She always wondered. Yet, that wasn't what puzzled her the most. Still, her classmates thought she was a bit too restrained for their liking; thus, in class, they would unprovokedly tap her shoulder and scream, "You and I after school mopping the floor with each other." She never understood why they always wanted to fight with her or initiate a conflict, as her reaction was always the same. Perhaps they thought they would get a different response if they provoked her enough, but she never did.

Zazi was a different breed; they could never grasp it, intensifying their anger. They couldn't understand why she couldn't simply be like them. So to avoid any drama after school, Zazi would flee into her transport, and she crowned a crowd for it, but she had gotten used to it, so she didn't care, and every other day, she would get home, take off her uniform then take Buhle off Tamara's hands, make sure his diapers were changed, fed him, bathed him, play with him for a while then make sure he sleeps that was the routine, barely even

14 playing Nanny McPhee. However, she loved caring for her baby brother, primarily when he would lie on her chest asleep, trying to syncopate her to how he was breathing so as not to wake him up. He had this thing of sucking his thumb as her uncle would, even though he didn't want anyone talking about it. She still hasn't gotten on with Tamara and couldn't comprehend her issue.

Zazi had become so fond of Buhle that she didn't even mind hiring a nanny; she adored being around him. Tamara was not the only one who seemed to have a grievance against her; Zazi was convinced that this nanny had been sent to test her patience, as she was consistently unkind to her without any apparent reason. It felt as though she harboured some ill will towards Zazi, as she always had something to say to or about her, which was concerning—where was she obtaining all that information? It couldn't have come from her grandfather, who rarely spoke with her, raising the question: could it be Sophie? She had hired her, after all. What could Sophie and Sinovuyo possibly be discussing regarding Zazi? She couldn't have been fabricating it.

So there was this particular day when Zazi had just returned from school. The nanny, Sinovuyo, was in the kitchen. Zazi, as always, rushed to see and kiss her baby brother. In her haste, she took off her shoes and left them near the cupboard in the kitchen, as she noticed that the lounge had been mopped and was still wet. She didn't want to dirty it with her shoes, so she tiptoed to the lounge. Before she knew it, Sinovuyo was breathing down her neck about it, saying, "Take these things of yours."
    Zazi: yes, I will
    Sinovuyo: when?
    Zazi: I said I'll take the shoes
    Sinovuyo: don't talk to me like that
    Zazi: like what?
    She picked up one of her school shoes and hurled it at her, striking Zazi in the face.
    Zazi: really?

Sinovuyo: you will respect me
Zazi: when did I ever disrespect you?

Rushing toward Zazi like an enraged rhino, she shoved her against the wall, seized and twisted her arm, slapped her across the face with her school shoes, and then dropped and struck her with the feather duster instead.

Sinovuyo: for someone that's a guest in this house, you sure have a big mouth

Zazi: Excuse me?

Nanny: I didn't stutter.

Zazi: what are you on about?

Sinovuyo Mr Richards and his wife have three children: Maurice, Christian, and Tamara. Currently, both Maurice and Christian are too young to have a child your age, and as for Tamara, she is just a teenager.

Zazi: okay?

At this point, Zazi couldn't believe her ears. She was utterly baffled by where she had been acquiring her information and the origin of her unpleasant attitude toward her.

Nanny: how on earth are you related here? Did they pull you out of a dumpster? Did you get adopted? Or are you merely some charity case?

Zazi: Mr. Richards is my grandpa

Nanny: No, he isn't. He only has three children, and I believe his granddaughter would prefer him not to be a parasite like you.

Zazi : parasite? Heh!

Nanny: You are merely here to exploit Mr Richards and his wife for their generosity.

Zazi was fuming; this woman was provoking her and pressing all the right buttons. Zazi, who had never liked being pushed, could no longer tolerate it.

Zazi: You don't even know anything. You act like you've got me all figured out or that we've figured it out, but you don't even know half of it.

Nanny: I doubt it

Zazi: Maurice is not my grandpa's child. Before they met, he was my grandmother's child, and my mother was Mr. Richard's firstborn. So yes, my grandpa does have three children, but Maurice is not one of them. If you haven't noticed, he is the only light-skinned person under this roof, whereas my grandpa isn't. The same goes for my grandmother, so he likely resembles his actual father, who isn't my grandpa by a million years.

Nanny: you are lying

Zazi: am I? You've been here like what? 2 seconds?

Nanny: how come I've never seen your mother? and nobody talks about her

Zazi: You should be asking whomever has been feeding you lies all this while

Sinovuyo couldn't believe her ears, and somehow, for some reason, she was furious. She opened the cupboard, grabbed a broom, and swung it towards Zazi, knocking things over and sending them tumbling across the room in an attempt to hit Zazi as she advanced, hoping to strike her unnoticed. But the moment she thought she had her, Zazi held both her hands, looked her in the eye, and shook her head in disappointment, disgust, and confusion as she pushed her away and walked to her room. Zazi was in her room, pondering what her grandmother must have against her or this Sinovuyo that they would go to such lengths and exchange lies. Sinovuyo, on the other hand, was the one she couldn't comprehend; she didn't even know her yet. She tried to snap out of it but couldn't as she buried herself in her homework, struggling to focus, reflecting on all the things she had confided in Sinovuyo and how that could land her in trouble. Perhaps she should report the matter to her grandfather, but that would only blow things out of proportion and might make matters worse.

It was Friday, and Zazi had just returned to the most prominent "Ta Da!" Yet her grandma was already home, preparing supper as she chopped the spinach. She appeared a bit broody and moody, rather angry. Zazi greeted her, saying, "Hey, Grandma." The silence responded so loudly that it raised the hairs on her neck. They stood still, her heart racing and her grandma's grip on the knife intensifying, her hands sweaty and slippery as she repositioned the spinach to chop at a better angle. Therefore, Zazi decided to walk backwards slowly, having never seen her grandma like this. She returned to her room, changed, and returned to the kitchen. After all, she was starving. She opened the bread bin but felt thirsty, so she moved to the other side of the sink and turned on the tap. Her grandma was cutting in slow motion but more loudly, and the silence couldn't have been more deadly. "Where did you get the nonsense you were spewing yesterday?"

Zazi: what?

Grandmother: you heard me

Zazi: I'm not following

Grandmother: Sinovuyo told me everything

Of course, she did—playing chess and not checkers, indeed. I thought to myself (she thought).

Zazi: what did she say I said?

Grandmother: That Maurice is not your grandfather's son

Zazi: uhmm…

Well, did I lie? So she thought but biting her tongue

Grandmother: You mentioned the little romance story of your grandfather and biological grandmother, how they dated, had a child, and I arrived and spoiled everything.

Zazi: I didn't, didn't…

Grandmother: you didn't what? Huh?

Zazi: I never said that

Grandmother: Then where did Sinovuyo hear it?

Zazi: I don't know, she twisted my words. She called me a leech, saying how much I hate you a lot, and I became annoyed trying to explain to her that I was family, as she didn't believe me. She claimed I was not even a part of this family and that I should be grateful. She insulted me and provoked me, so I got angry and started telling her that I am who I say I am.

Grandmother: so you expect me to believe you?

Zazi: no, just don't believe her

Grandmother: Do you believe me then? I always knew you hated me, but I never expected it to be like this. Why wouldn't you address Maurice as an uncle? Is it because he isn't your grandfather's child? Is that why you hate me? Do you think I separated your grandparents? Well, let me tell you something: they had been long separated when I came into your granddad's life. I don't even know what your biological grandmother looks like.

Zazi didn't know why or how, but she felt an overwhelming guilt as tears streamed down her face, attempting to explain herself and apologise.

Grandmother: I'm not mad at you, child, just disappointed. Now get out of my face.

Zazi: I'm sorry; I have nothing against you. I couldn't hate you; you are the only mother I've ever known in my entire life.

Grandmother: well, you would do well to remember that, now move!

Zazi walked away, trying not to anger her grandma further, wiping the tears streaming down her face. She couldn't understand why she felt so guilty and yet so sorry, and also why her grandma wanted Zazi to pretend that Maurice was indeed her grandfather's child; it wasn't as if her husband was making a great effort to make it seem like Maurice was his child; after all, he wasn't. She threw herself onto her bed, burying her face in her pillow, wishing the earth could swallow her whole and Maurice and Tamara wouldn't hear about this, as she wasn't ready to repeat her conversation with her grandma. Still, alas, Tamara was already pressing her about it, asking why she had never referred to him as an uncle or addressed him after Maurice returned from the mountain. When Christian returned, even though he was younger, she knew to call him uncle. Zazi couldn't, and she tried to refrain from answering, knowing that no matter what she said, they would twist her words against her…

"Grandpa instructed me," she yelled without blinking. Immediately after letting her tongue slip, she regretted it; this was likely never to be repeated… and she knew.

Eight

Family Ties and Fault Lines

"Family ties can bind tightly, but they can also suffocate."
"Family is a double-edged sword—it can wound as deeply as it can heal."

Zazi thought it would be a long time before 2015 ended, but to her surprise, it happened in the blink of an eye; the year was done and dusted. It was still December, though, but that didn't matter, seeing as schools and churches were closed. Shopping had already been crossed off her "to-do list." Her uncle Christian was home for the holidays as always, the one person she adored, and so was Maurice (Mo). Maurice being home made no difference, at least not to Zazi, as they were as good as strangers.

Zazi had been experiencing numerous changes ever since she returned. She had been feeling deep, uncontrollable urges that she had no idea how to handle or what they meant. Still, according to the Bible, every other Sunday at church was sinful as she was supposed to live by the spirit and not otherwise. Oh, and she had started her periods around the 14th of July, right after they had been taught about menstruation at school, which, according to her teachers, should have been explained at home. At first, before it happened, she felt excited. However, she never anticipated the "perks" that came with it—the constant paranoia of whether she had stained herself and the discomfort associated with the pads, which felt like diapers. The awful smell, the disgusting blood clots that escaped her vaginal area, reeking of something foul. Moreover, the directive to "close your legs" came more angrily and was much more frequent now from her grandma's lips all day, along with the constant refrain to "sit like a lady."

She wondered if boys were ever taught to "sit like a gentleman." In any case, she couldn't help but be taken aback by her grandma's command. She had just turned 13, but even so, she was still no lady, merely a child, and therefore, she ought to have been free to sit however she pleased. 2015 had come to an end, and she would be starting the seventh grade the following year.

It is astonishing how even what seems like endless years can pass in an instant, especially when no one is keeping track. For the holidays, she was supposed to be in Lady Frere; instead, she had to return to Cape Town as Victoria popped another cherry. According to her, Zazi's presence was required at Home Affairs, being the big sister and all, which was surprisingly odd. However, this occurred earlier, around August. Zazi had left Cape Town only to arrive and discover that there was no emergency at all. Emergency; her dear mother simply wanted to rendezvous while Zazi sat… Well, not with the newborn, just her now 5-year-old sibling, as the new bundle she carried wherever she decided to vanish into thin air.

Everything happened in haste, making her wonder what was going through her mother's mind when she decided to be here, as there was no need for her. Still, as always, she had to be the adult in the situation, regardless of how panicked she felt; Byron's presence made her uneasy, and her mother wouldn't have it any other way, as she trusted Byron rather than her child. Clenching her teeth and buttocks as Byron advanced towards her again, she attempted to decline subtly, but he wouldn't allow it. "Why are you acting all brand new? As if you don't enjoy it."

If only he knew how cringe-worthy he made her feel, but of course, he must have, given how he threatened her and left her battered to sway and dismay her from revealing the truth. As if she could ever tell anyone—who would even listen anyway? "Open your legs?" he ordered with a smug grin as he parted her legs, one going east and the other west. Zazi tightened her grip on the sheets, eyes shut, just hoping to die so this misery could end. She tried so hard to be unbothered by what was happening as her body shut down, tears streaming down her cheeks, leaving the pillow drenched.

Holding her breath, hoping she would die with every stroke and wishing it were her last. After having his way with her tirelessly, as usual, he passed out and slept like a baby. Zazi fidgeted beside him, quietly hoping he wouldn't wake. She began to detach herself from him, leaping from Victoria's bed and crawling slowly into hers, which stood at the other corner of the room. She barely slept a wink as she held her body in disgust, asking and blaming herself, "Why did I even agree to come here again?"

Hardly sleeping, Byron woke to her silently sobbing, but he cared little as he hurried to get dressed, claiming he had to leave early. "Come and close the door," she said. She approached without making a sound, yet ultimately walked him out through the gate, her expression intense and wildly enraged, his large eyes wide with terror as he faced a barrage of demands. Some of them went along the lines of, "If you happen to get pregnant, go to a clinic and have an abortion." She just agreed, "The condom might have burst." Now, feeling panicked and anxious, she thought, Why would the condom burst? What was he doing with her, to begin with? What had he done to her? Her mind was darting from one thought to another, and her eyes scanned up, down, and sideways. "DO YOU UNDERSTAND?!" he yelled, but quietly, she merely nodded as he nearly crushed her wrist yet still held on and didn't let go. "Yes, I understand now. Let me go," she said, attempting to free her wrist from his grasp. He regarded her with hatred, pity, and anger, instilling fear in her eyes as she watched him walk away. She staggered inside, her in-betweens burning and aching, and just as she was about to close the door behind her, Victoria waltzed in. Looking surprised, she had never expected her this early—no greeting, not even a simple "Hey, you slept well," just a ...

Victoria: Where's Byron? Did he come last night
and, of course, that would be the first thing she asks about
Zazi: yes, why?
Victoria: why's he not here? I can't see him.
Zazi: last time I checked, he didn't live here.
Victoria: yes! But there wasn't a reason for him to leave early.
Zazi: hilarious
Victoria: unless you know why he left so early
Zazi: I don't
Victoria: what was that?
Zazi: nothing!
Victoria: if you see him, tell him I said thank you
Zazi: (I wonder why) sure thing!

She disappeared again; that was the last Zazi saw of her that day. However, in the evening, Byron was back flirting with Amile, demanding that she twerk for him, spanking her all the while and giving Zazi a mean, intense look that haunted her with night terrors. While kissing Amile and trying to finger her, looking at Zazi, Amile admittedly tried to get away from him, but he wouldn't let go. Although Zazi couldn't tell from where she stood whether she liked it or was merely trying not to appear "uptight", whatever the case, she wished they would chase and thirst for each other elsewhere rather than behind her mother's door in her house. That was rather disrespectful. What did Byron understand about respect? To protect her sanity, Zazi had to leave them be and find somewhere else where she wouldn't see or hear any of this, but she couldn't, as the air escaped her and her lungs started to shut down. It felt like the walls were closing in on her. As she pounded her chest like a gorilla, hoping that would somehow help get air into her lungs while she struggled against her nostrils for even a tiny bit of breath, she couldn't afford to appear weak or affected, especially not in front of him. Thus, she had to compose herself, gathering her strength and breath. By the time Zazi returned, Amile was fastening her skirt and adjusting her attire. As I entered, she appeared startled, looking down at her toes with one hand resting on the opposite shoulder. She couldn't even raise her head as she pleaded.

"I have to go home."

Byron: no, you don't

Amile: yes, I do. It's late, and my mom will wonder where I am

Byron: no, she won't. You live right In front. She knows where you are

Zazi: could you guys take this elsewhere

Byron: shut up

Zazi: This is inappropriate

Byron: lol, jealous?

Zazi: eeuw!

Amile: well, I have to go

As he grabbed her from behind, she attempted to escape his clutches; however, as was often the case, he could not accept a No. He simply had to have it his way. His dark hands glided along her coconut inner thighs, seeking her panties as she persistently denied him. As Nwabisa walked in abruptly, she paused at the door as if something had swallowed her foot. Her jaw dropped, and she mopped the floor, but subtly, she pressed her lips together to avoid making a fuss. Byron's eyes darted from corner to corner until the door seemed eager to welcome his next project, something to engage with.

Zazi was the least excited as he attempted his tricks with Nwabisa, but she wouldn't flinch. A clever girl, she had balls more significant than a bull's, and of course, she did; she had a tsunami for a mother and was, therefore, well-trained for the crisis, unlike the rest of us. As we discussed, we were swept away, allowing Smile to escape while Byron stood in astonishment, unsure how to handle being turned down. Zazi and Nwabisa couldn't care less as he stood up, stormed out, and left. They walked outside, and some random boys were throwing stones. Who did that? And for what reason? As much as Zazi wanted to retreat to her chambers, her "friends" appeared to favour the skinny little heartbreakers that had stood before them.

Zazi never understood why her peers rushed for things like love in their youth instead of focusing on education and simply enjoying being children. Watching them go back and forth with these boys, witnessing their fraternising and feeling relieved that she no longer had to live here, kicking stones and wondering when each of their tongues would return to its original throats. With much on her mind and plate, her memory was somewhat hazy as she could not recall Victoria returning that night or why she had dragged her to Cape Town again apart from her excuses. Despite everything that occurred, being away for weeks while schools remained open and missing the third term exams, she still managed to pass and return home just before the holidays.

When she returned, she travelled from Cape Town to Lady Frere. With little happening, the holidays seemed to fly by quickly yet slowly for Zazi, as she was eager to be rid of Victoria. Although it appeared that she couldn't get her out of her hair for a while, she decided to make herself scarce from Victoria and Zara, who would tail her around as she bit her head off and told her off. Zazi always felt like an animal when her sister was trying to get close to her big sister. Even so, Zazi couldn't look beyond Victoria's betrayal and all the other wrongs her stepdad and Byron committed every time she laid eyes on her sister.

She had so much rage and disgust within herself that she couldn't comprehend it. It reminded her of her relationship with her aunt Tamara, whom she had always loved and longed to connect with. Yet, all she received was a cold shoulder and silence; she was never acknowledged but merely ordered about. Even though it wasn't what she wanted or needed, she was still grateful that she recognised her at least. Until one particular day, years before Victoria chose to crawl back into her life, she must have been eight.

That day, it was just Tamara and Zazi at home. She woke up, and the house felt empty as if everyone had been sucked into oblivion, leaving her with the wicked witch aunt. She stood in the middle of the passage while Tamara slapped and ducked her, crashing to the floor and landing on her chest with no hint of mercy in sight. Tamara yanked out her foot and pressed it down her face, feeling Zazi feeling the carpet burns on her cheek, then helping her to her feet just to kick and punch her in the face, continuously kissing the wall behind her, choking and screaming at her for answers she could not give and questions she couldn't understand kicking her to the curb as she choked on air barely breathing or being given the room landing on the floor yet again feeling as if a rib or two was broken as she kept on hitting until she couldn't anymore. Zazi didn't know when she collapsed, falling unconscious on the floor. She had always been physically weak. With all those flashbacks, every time she looked at her sister, she felt as if she were becoming her or, worse still, Victoria, or perhaps the worst aspects of both of them. She was punishing her sister for things beyond her control, but she simply had to vent. Eventually, the holidays ended, and Victoria returned to Cape Town with her children.

Nine

Crossroads of Choice

"*Every choice comes with a price, but some decisions are the initial steps towards freedom.*"

"*When you find yourself at the crossroads, the most challenging choice is not the correct path—it's having the courage to take the first step.*"

Another chapter is complete, turning the page and starting a new chapter filled with resolutions for the new year. Although Santa never came by with Zazi's gifts, he must have been very particular about his presents or perhaps just running late. Zazi thought to herself as she hoped that God or whoever didn't have any more surprises in store this year, for all she ever wished for was peace. School reopening marked her final year in primary school (Louis Rex). After returning from Lady Frere, she set her luggage down in the passageway, hugged her grandmother, and then went to her room. However, she couldn't step further as she stood in awe, wondering if she was even in the right house. Her room and bed were occupied by unfamiliar faces, to say the least. As she greeted them with an "afternoon," an unwilling voice replied with a lacklustre "Hi." Oh, how enthusiastic and charming! It appeared her new roommates had an attitude and were rather grumpy, prompting her to attempt to break the awkward silence...

Zazi: how are you?

Stranger 1: Good, and you?

Zazi: I'm well, thanks; uhm, am I in the wrong room?

Stranger: no, I don't think so. We are new here

Zazi: I know

Stranger: although we've met before

Zazi: oh, have we now?

Stranger: yes! I'm Anton from Mount Frere

Zazi: Anton? Hmm, as in my grandmother's home town?

Anton: yes! She's my aunt

Zazi: oh! Nice to meet you, I suppose

Anton: likewise, do you remember me/ us now?

Zazi: I can't say sorry if you'll excuse

Anton: of course

She left the room to find her grandmother, wondering why she hadn't been informed and what they were doing in her room. Before she could utter a word, it was as though her grandmother had read her mind.

Granny: You must have seen the twins in your

Zazi: uhm twins?

Granny: yes! Amanda and Anton

Zazi: oh, had I no idea they were twins, but yes, I saw them

Granny: what do you mean?

Zazi: I didn't know

Granny: you have met them before. They are my Sister Claudine's Kids

Zazi: well, I think I remember Claudine. I can't say I remember her kids. I'm sorry

Granny: they stayed with my mother back at home, but I decided to bring them here; the education on that side is lacking, so...

Zazi: I see

Granny: I trust you guys will get along well

Zazi: well, I hope so

Observing how rude and self-centred this Amanda character was, she felt uncertain. This would be the first time she had stayed under the same roof as her peers, let alone in the same room.

Granny: you guys are around the same age, so you should

Zazi: probably (although she wasn't so sure about that)

Granny: I hope you are hungry because there's food in the microwave

Zazi: well, I'm famished; oh, for me?

Granny: yes

Zazi: you knew I was coming?

Granny: Eventually, yes, but the food was initially for Amanda, but she wouldn't eat it so you can have it.

Zazi: Okay, are you sure she won't eat it or want it?

Granny: no, I'm not sure, but there's no shortage of food in this house, so she can always have something else

Zazi: Okay

She walked to the microwave, took her food, and went straight to the lounge. Tamara was there; she greeted her. As always, she ignored me. After finishing her food, something about the atmosphere made her feel like a guest in what was supposed to be her home. She needed some fresh air, but for an empty house, it felt crowded as everywhere was occupied. The lounge was complete, her room was unwelcoming, and she couldn't just relax in other people's rooms or follow her grandmother around as if she didn't know her way about the house. Even though there was another lounge, she couldn't sit there either, as it was meant for visitors and always had to be kept clean.

Zazi was pacing back and forth, trying to figure out what to do as she felt bored. Amanda walked by looking furious; she dashed up and down the kitchen, pulling out pots and some vegetables from the fridge. It seemed like she was about to prepare and cook supper, which, for some reason, stirred something in Zazi. Zazi chose to leave her to her cooking in the kitchen and instead went to their room. There were three of them in the room, and although it was the largest room in the house, it somehow felt cramped for

Zazi. Or perhaps she had become accustomed to being alone ever since Thelma and Lyla left.

Anton was playing games in the room, so Zazi joined him. He was a fun and laid-back lad compared to his twin. After chatting with Anton, she realised she knew them but hadn't seen them in a while; after all, she hadn't been to Mount Fletcher in some time, and they had never come here before. Despite knowing her grandmother, Zazi didn't quite like villages. She hardly ever goes home; even when she does, it always looks like she's running away from something. Even when we were at Lady Frere, she never stayed long, but she had to be there as the family's "bride," even if she didn't want to follow tradition.

As she spoke to Anton, she realised that she shouldn't take Amanda seriously—at least, that's what Anton advised. Yet she still couldn't wrap her head around the fact that she also had to share her bed with this person, even though she acted as if they were mortal enemies. She couldn't understand her problem, but she knew she couldn't sleep in the same bed as someone who looked at her disgusted, as if she had done something wrong.

Amanda walked in while Anton and Zazi were in the midst of a conversation. She must have finished cooking. She looked furious. Zazi couldn't comprehend, but she recalled that Anton had advised her to ignore Amanda, so she tried to until Amanda intervened in their conversation and decided to escalate things. She somehow took offence even when no one was speaking to or about her. From Zazi's perspective, it seemed as though Amanda thrived on drama, and if she couldn't find any, she felt compelled to create it. A true chaos maker, she began to insult Zazi, leaving Zazi in shock, unsure of what to do or say. She attempted to ignore Amanda, but when irritated, Amanda said something that prompted Zazi to respond. Amanda repeatedly asked, "What did you just say?" Zazi wasn't going to repeat herself, trying to minimise the already escalating drama.
    Zazi: I said what I said

Amanda: you wouldn't dare repeat it
Zazi: I would, but I would rather not
Anton: chill out, Amanda. It was but a joke
Amanda: this has nothing to do with you
Anton: sure it does; it just never involved you
Zazi: exactly!
Anton was laughing, and Zazi just giggled
Amanda: you are laughing?
Zazi: would you rather have me cry?
Anton: quit being a bully
Amanda: well, she should stop tempting me
Zazi: I was never even trying to

As Amanda charged towards her, going complete Hulk, she slammed her hands onto Zazi's face, sending her off her backside and onto her back on the mattress. Zazi immediately sat up, clutching her stinging cheek, and smiled. Amanda was fuming even more. She kept poking Zazi's forehead, causing it to jerk back and forth violently, provoking her into a fight.

Amanda: don't you dare disrespect me
Zazi: just stop it
Amanda: or what?
Zazi: just stop, please
Amanda: oh, but I like it
Zazi: well, it's not funny
Amanda: I'm not trying to be a sweetheart. Now quit being a coward and fight me.
Zazi: No

As she was getting what she wanted, she became furious and began slapping Zazi repeatedly; she could no longer maintain her composure and wished to silence Amanda. Zazi stood up and struck her unexpectedly as she got to her feet, knocking her off balance and challenging her arrogance, but her rage refused to dissipate. She sprang back up, attempting to swing at Zazi but missed as Zazi held her hand and said, "Just stop. I don't want to fight you," yet Amanda wouldn't back down. Eventually, Zazi grew weary and retaliated again, sending her hefty frame flying across the room, landing on the mirror and shaking it off its stand.

Still not backing down, she hurled herself at Zazi and began throwing punches, so Zazi simply allowed her to have her way while she shielded her face. After a while, Anton intervened and put a stop to the altercation. However, Amanda was far from pleased, as she refused to climb off Zazi, shouting, "I told you not to mess with me." Zazi, being Zazi, chose to disregard her and left her to it. It was evident to her instantly that she would need to sleep with one eye open.

As this was a war for Amanda, she had become her new nemesis. When it was time to sleep, Amanda wouldn't stop hogging the blankets and pulling them, causing Zazi to get cold and freeze during the night. Zazi ceased trying to pull the blankets towards her and let Amanda have them. As they slept soundly, a loud noise suddenly echoed through the house walls: "iBBE EYONDLAYO EKUSENI," announced Mafabhavuma on Mhlobo and Wenene FM. Shortly after, there was a knock at the door twice, followed by footsteps that faded into the kitchen. It was past 5 am. On a school morning, as usual, Zazi woke Anton as she left to bathe. She brushed her teeth and returned to her room to get dressed, as that's where her uniform was. She wore her socks and shoes, tied her braids, looked in the mirror momentarily, and headed to the kitchen. As always, she greeted her grandpa, saying, "Morning, Grandpa," when he had already prepared breakfast at the dining table. "Sit down and eat," he said.

Zazi: you made me breakfast?

Grandpa: yes, but I forgot it's no longer just the two of us

Zazi: well, of course, thank you

She took the bowl, made her way to the table, pulled out a chair, and sat down, despite how difficult it was to function in the morning after eating. Richards attempted to spark a conversation, as he never liked his granddaughter being quiet; he kept asking her questions, but Zazi was so lost in her thoughts that she hardly heard him. "Is something the matter?"

Zazi: what? Why would there be anything wrong?

Grandpa: just asking…slept well?

Zazi: Well, I slept

Grandpa: I see

Zazi: yeah

Grandpa: so, how are you finding the twins

Zazi: okay, I guess

Grandpa: I see

Zazi: yeah, all good

Grandpa: So, are you getting along well?

Zazi: Why wouldn't we be?

Grandpa: no reason, I suppose. I just need to make sure

Zazi: I see

Zazi disliked every moment of this conversation. She had to finish her breakfast in haste, as she didn't want to appear as a snitch, as if she couldn't manage her affairs or dislike Amanda. She believed that keeping it from her granddad was the best option. At the same time, she wondered why there was a sudden interest; her granddad only ever asked questions like this when he suspected something or already knew what was happening, yet he still probed because he hoped for some honesty. Nevertheless, she couldn't provide it this time, which felt like she was giving him the cold shoulder.

"excuse me, please."

Grandpa: by all means

He gazed at her with worry in his eyes. Zazi needed to check how far Anton and Amanda were, as everything regarding her grandpa had to be done on time. Mr Anton was finished; he only needed to eat. In contrast, Amanda hadn't even bathed and chose to sleep instead. Mr Richards was unimpressed as time passed swiftly, and she was showered slower than a snail, showing no care in the world.

Grandpa: you still haven't bathed?

Amanda: Well, I'm going to

Grandpa: have you seen the time

Amanda: yes, I have

Grandpa: so, does it look convenient to be bathing at this hour when I woke you all up at 5 am

Amanda: I didn't know

Grandpa: Zazi and Anton had no problem knowing that, so what's your excuse?

Amanda: I better go and bath or else I might never

Grandpa: right

Mr. Richards felt disrespected. He thought he would have his hands complete with Amanda as if Zazi weren't enough. He went to brush his teeth and encountered Zazi there. Observing Amanda's attitude and knowing his granddaughter, he was curious.

Grandpa: why didn't you wake Amanda up?

Zazi: I didn't know I was supposed to

Grandpa: well, you sleep in the same bed

Zazi: yes, and because of it, I thought she heard the knock or the radio, at least, so I woke Anton up instead

Grandpa: I see, well you better clean up here; I'll bring the car around

Zazi: yes, sir!

Grandpa: Tell Anton and Amanda I don't want to be late

Grandpa: sure

He stepped out of the bathroom, Zazi, and tidied up, wiping the sink and turning off the taps, ensuring everything was as it had been. She had a wee before leaving and went to find Anton in the dining room. "Let's go. Grandpa doesn't want to be late."

Anton: Amanda's still getting dressed

Zazi: she's what?

Anton: still getting dressed
Zazi: She better make haste; see you outside

Zazi stopped and headed towards the garage. Her grandpa's Toyota Hilux twin cab was no longer there, so she closed the gates behind her, but not entirely, as Anton came rushing up from behind.
Anton: wait
She smiled, assuring him she would not lock the car and got inside.
Grandpa: where's the chubby one?
Zazi: who? Amanda?
Grandpa: yes!
Zazi: coming, I suppose
Grandpa: well, she better hurry, or I'm leaving
Concerned and knowing her grandpa, Zazi had to ask Anton or find Amanda herself.
Zazi: where's Amanda?
Anton: last I checked, she was still getting dressed
Zazi: Grandpa wants to leave
Anton: well, he should leave, we should all leave, and she can walk
Zazi: seriously?
Anton: yes! Amanda might be my twin, but she's also the most selfish person I know.
Zazi: doesn't matter.
Anton: Get inside the car. Will she come or not? Either way, we shouldn't wait for her.
As Anton instructed, she returned to the car, trying to comprehend how these two could be twins. Their indifference towards one another was astonishing.
Mr Richards was exasperated by the wait for her, so he backed up the car, hoping she might come racing after him. Amanda simply stood there, challenging him to abandon her….

Ten

Forgiveness as Liberation

"Forgiveness is not a sign of weakness; it is the bravery to let go of what restrains you." "Forgiveness is not a pardon for others but a release for yourself."

So, after what felt like a prolonged process, Zazi finally arrived at school as she was the last one to be dropped off. Mr Richards handed her pocket money and wished her good luck and a good day as Zazi stepped out of the car and watched him swerve away, fading into the distance. Standing in front of the gate once more at the beginning of another year made her reminisce about how she had stood there last year, dreading going inside while the schoolchildren crawled in and out like a hive of bees.

She couldn't wait to finish the school calendar, and for a moment, she thought the other pupils would attack her, but she got used to it. Since, like Talfalah, they had no school ball or anyone else to gather for assembly in front of the classes, they stood every Monday, especially when school reopened. To pray, announce awards, discuss the good and the bad that transpired, and listen to the principal preach on and on while half the school fell asleep, standing there for what felt like an eternity.

After assembly, every learner was assigned to their respective classes and new grades, while some remained anchored to the same class and grade as the previous year and even for several years. Everyone proceeded to their designated classes and took their seats as their new teacher greeted them. A tall, dark, and elegant lady entered Zazi's class. She had dreadlocks that she had dyed black, and she wore long heels which suited her already tall stature. Her confidence overshadowed some men's egos. She possessed a fierce, sexy, and classy appearance. Her elegance spoke volumes as she entered the room quietly, her heels clicking and clacking behind her. She stood in the middle of the class and exhaled.

"you may all be seated, and you are already seated."

Since they were already seated, they stood up and greeted, "Good morning, ma'am."

"Okay! Thank you for your silence, and by all means louder, please let the whole world know you are here."

The whole class kept quiet.

Voice: Thank you! Now, where was I? Ah yes, I am Mrs Mfamana. I am married, have three children, and adore my wonderful husband. I am a family-oriented woman. I love teaching, so let's hope you enjoy learning and studying as much as I cherish my job …

The class fell silent, stunned. They could see this woman meant business and that they had to be on their best behaviour. Zazi couldn't help but admire her. It was as if they were all seeing her for the first time. She had never taught some of Zazi's classmates like she had Zazi, but some had, which gave them ample reasons to love and hate her yet still respect her by any means necessary.

"Right, let's finish the introductions to kick off the day. You're ready! Let's keep it brief and pleasant." Zazi felt a chill run down her spine. She despised introductions; they frightened her to bits. She suffered from social anxiety, was antisocial, a loner, and an introvert. The introductions commenced from the first row to the left as one entered through the door...

Student: Good morning, ma'am, and good morning, class. My name is Olivia North. I am 13 years old, and I live in Nomzamo. I love people, so thank you!

As she sat down, the class applauded. *Yuck, who loves people? She must be out of her mind,* Zazi thought to herself.

Student 2: Hello. My name is Shona North, and I am Olivia's brother. We live in the same house, and I love football. Thank you!

He sat down, appearing somewhat embarrassed and slightly out of breath. Zazi's eyes darted from face to face, trying to see if anyone else felt as fearful of being a witness if they sensed her fear. It was now her turn. She could feel her insides twist as corpses do in their graves.

Zazi: Greetings. I am Zazi Richards, residing in the suburban area of Westbourne. I have a passion for art, reading, music, and learning. Thank you.

She said as she sat down. The introductions were completed in what felt like a flash. Mrs Mfamana was pleased, as she could now proceed with her demands, of which she appeared to have an extensive list.

Mrs Mfamana: I'm not sure you know, but I am your class teacher. This is my class, and I expect you all to be obedient, as I'm not particularly fond of disorderly behaviour. In addition to teaching you natural science, I'm also the music instructor here, and I hope my very own class will make up the majority of my choir.

And there she went, suddenly startling Zazi somewhat. "Whatever happened to a show of hands or volunteering?" Zazi pondered to herself. She didn't like this one bit, as her hand was already being forced. As it was the first day at school and a bit chaotic, the students only had to sit still, remain quiet, keep themselves occupied, and avoid getting into any mischief.

The scholars were likely to receive their timetable sometime during the week, as the teachers remained busy with other commitments. Some students were merely attempting to obtain the stationery list or were planning to purchase it now, which raises the question of what they've been waiting for all this time. As soon as Mrs Mfamana left the classroom, the students began to scatter, some remaining within the school grounds to see which classes their friends and peers were in and to get some fresh air.

A class of fifty with twenty-five desks was suddenly almost empty within minutes as students bolted. Zazi peeks through the window and sees how practically the entire school is scattered across the playground, and there is no sign of teachers as they are all secured in the staff room, well, some of them, anyway. Mrs Mfamana returned from the staff room to check on her class, and thankfully, she never noticed that some students were missing, or perhaps she just didn't want to make a fuss about it. Zazi felt uneasy, thinking, what if Mrs Mfamana did notice and asked her? She wasn't one to lie, nor was she a snitch, with thoughts racing back and forth but pausing every time their class teacher stepped out.

She exhaled and murmured, "Thank God, that was close." After a long day of sitting and doing nothing, school had just ended, and quite early too, but it was still the first day of "BACK TO SCHOOL." Walking out of the school gate, she realised her grandpa was supposed to pick her up. However, she couldn't find his car amidst the chaos as she paced up and down outside the school grounds, looking tired and annoyed. Feeling the burning sensation from the heated ground seeping through her shoes, she endured cars hooting and honking, children screaming and shouting, and cars arriving and leaving. The fumes made Zazi nauseous, the noise dizzying her, and the heat draining every ounce of water and energy within her. She stretched her neck like an ostrich, searching for her grandpa amongst the throng of cars while being jostled from side to side by fellow students rushing out of the gate.

As she looked down at her shoes, wiping the sweat from her face, it felt like it was melting away. She noticed a shadow and some strange adult shoes. Someone was standing before her, so she tilted her head up; the person wore heavy-looking trousers that seemed to be sagging from the waist down. She didn't understand why he wouldn't move or step aside and instead stood there as she raised her chin to see this man.

"I've been calling and hooting non-stop; your grandfather said to come to pick you up."

"Oh, apologies, I had no idea. May I ask why?"

"Well, he said he was running late and might be unable to pick up on time. He doesn't want you here stranded."

"Alright then, let's go."

They made their way to the man's car. He was a friend of her grandad or a retired colleague. They both worked at the Department of Agriculture in Lady Frere, but Mr. Dambuza had retired at sixty and was now living on a pension. On her way home, there was dead silence in the car before she realised they had arrived. "We are here," he said. "I'll call your grandad and let him know."

"Alright, thanks," Zazi said

As she stepped out of the car, closed the door behind her, opened the gate, and approached the front door, she realised she couldn't find the keys, so she rang the doorbell. Precious appeared and handed her the keys. She unlocked the door, entered, and saw Mr. Dambuza driving away as he honked goodbye. She left her bag near the outside bathroom door in the passage, used the toilet, and then hurried to the kitchen to find something to eat.

There were leftovers, cheese, juice, bread in the bread bin, butter, and everything else, so she took all of it. But first, she downed a bottle of Long Life. After feasting and feeling like her tummy was about to explode, she had to sit down and catch her breath as she entered the living room. The house was relatively quiet. Tamara was at school, returning to improve her grade 12 marks. Anton and Amanda were at school, too; her grandpa was still at work, and so was her grandmother. It was just Precious, Buhle's new nanny.

She wasn't sure what else to do, so she decided to sleep in her room. She watched the plate and cup she had used in the sink, then went to her room, removed her uniform, and sat there for a while before falling asleep. Waking up every other day and returning from school, her days were pretty much the same, except that homework and assignments seemed to increase. Amanda and Tamara are inseparable best friends, so at least she still has Anton in her corner. Sophie still does Zazi's laundry every other weekend and also irons her uniform. Yet, Zazi couldn't help but feel guilty for not cooking or cleaning, let alone doing her laundry. Everything was done for her, whereas Amanda, who was only a year older, did everything for herself. According to her grandmother, Amanda was used to it because she had to manage everything for herself and everyone, including her uncles.

Mr. Richards was still the same, nagging Sophie about Zazi doing her laundry and whatnot, but her grandma wouldn't tolerate it. Then came a particular weekend when everything almost seemed normal, yet one person was absent from lunch, dinner, and supper. Sophie and her husband wondered where their dear daughter could be. Then the doorbell rang, and she walked in as if being shoved, almost as if possessed. She brushed past her mother, who was poised to give her a piece of her mind, and headed straight for her room; Sophie followed her. She wouldn't allow it today. She dragged her reluctant feet across the mat, forcing her legs to comply as she wandered towards her room, mere seconds away from the kitchen. "Tamara, what is the meaning of this?" Sophie demanded.

"Quiet, you are too loud", she answered

The audacity of her

"Tamara, I'm talking to you."

"No, you are screaming at me …"

"Do not mock me, child."

"I need to sleep, so if you'll excuse me."

Sophie, infuriated by Christian and her contradictory instincts, was being tested, and she wasn't about to let the devil win, at least not this night. She found herself torn between her unwavering support for her child, which she had consistently defended and excused even when wrong. In Tam's steadfast support for her children's eyes, this felt like enabling her bad behaviour and awarding her gold medals instead of providing proper discipline.

At this point, Sophie didn't know what to do; however, she also didn't want to feel weak or unable to manage her child. The disappointment and embarrassment towards her daughter made it difficult for her to let go of the situation, compelling her to punish her. She swung her arm, causing Tamara to land on her behind, and before she could protest, another slap struck her face, leaving her angry, panting, and sober. Yet, she didn't stop there. Sophie continued to deliver blows as though they were shots at a bar, declaring, "I will not be disrespected, not in my own house and certainly not by you." At this moment, Tamara dared not retort any longer. It was probably due to the alcohol. Mr Richards stood quietly, arms folded, no doubt telling himself to stay out of it as he made his way to her room.

The last time Mr Richards attempted to discipline Tamara, she was never at home and only returned when she realised her mother was coming back. This indicated her lack of respect for her father. Despite his efforts to set her straight, she later had police at his doorstep, and it was rumoured that Sophie advised Tamara to do this, claiming that her husband had no right to lay a hand on Tamara when he had never even reprimanded Victoria. But then again, how could he? He had never raised her. Unlike Tamara, her father was unaware of Victoria's mischief, and in any case, she was never away from home, at least not when her father was around. Sophie burst into Tamara's room, grabbed Buhle, and thrust him into Tamara's arms, saying, "Take your child, and he better not cry." As she gently placed him on the bed, her eyes wide with intensity, Sophie was silently screaming things she had no business hearing. At the same time, Amanda laughed heartily with a judgmental look on her face, searching for further things to penalise, as if this charade wasn't enough. Zazi decided to retreat to her room, as this entire situation was becoming too much, and she disliked drama. She stumbled upon Amanda and Anton discussing the matter. Anton appeared displeased and disappointed while his cousin Tamara argued with Amanda, who exclaimed, "How shameless can she be?"

Weren't they supposed to be all tongue and saliva? At least, that's what Zazi thought. Now, she wasn't so confident about Amanda. She seemed more like a slithering reptile than a family member. As Zazi prepared for bed, Sophie walked in and demanded that they all listen.
"Zazi!"
"Grandma?"
"I don't care what Tamara says to you. Don't you dare take that baby tonight"
"Okay, but what if he cries like right now ?"
"That's not your problem; you are but a child; therefore, let her mind her baby."
"Okay, grandma"
"And I'm not just talking to Zazi, but the lot of you as well; I don't want anyone in that room, no matter how much that baby cries."
"Yes, aunt!"
She banged the door shut on her way out, and Buhle screamed and wailed the whole night. After a while, it went quiet, and he must have fallen asleep.

Eleven

Whisper of Hope

"When you stand at the edge of despair, hope is the whisper urging you not to jump."

"Even in the darkest hours, there is a faint whisper: you are not finished yet."

Days passed after that incident with Tamara. Even weeks went by, and one would think she would have at least gained some wisdom, but no. She didn't come home drunk again, but she still showed no interest in her child, giving him the exact look she once gave Zazi. At least now, Zazi can find comfort knowing she was never the problem. Zazi and Amanda were always misaligned. Mr Richards was constantly working, and so was Sophie. Zazi and Anton continued to get along, and their bond grew more assertive.

The school was much like Zazi; her classmates were always causing trouble, and she often was caught in the crossfire. Most teachers were becoming increasingly furious and frustrated with Zazi's class, 7c, now more than ever. Although her class wasn't the only one giving the teachers a headache, all the

English 7th graders (7c, 7d, and 7e) posed more of a challenge than 7a and 7b, which were considered well-behaved from the teachers' perspectives. The Afrikaans classes 7a and 7b were much smaller and kinder.

The fun only lasted a short while. As usual, they all went to the canteen to get food on this particular day, typically before 10 a.m. or after the first break. That would have been tea time if they had been employees instead of students. By the time they reached the canteen, it was a mess. Food had flooded the school grounds as they allowed the aunties to dish up for them, which they then threw on the floor, decorating the walls. It was repulsive.

They served food to Zazi and her class. The other students from different classes behaved as though hooligans were vandalising the entire school. While they were acting out, Zazi, noticing the expressions on their faces, realised the food was inedible as it was passed along to others who might have been hungry enough to eat anything. Zazi, however, had been taught never to look a gift horse in the mouth, so she simply ate her food. At the same time, some of her classmates laughed and couldn't believe she could consume such a thing. As soon as she finished, she dashed over to the tap. She stretched her neck as she leaned towards the tap's spout, hoping to wash away the taste lingering in her mouth, but it was never that easy. Soon after, 7c returned there after they had finished feasting.

During the Maths period in Mrs Bolani's class, who was also the deputy principal, she was not present initially. She vanished right after the lesson began once they entered her classroom. After they were all seated and returned from the canteen, two kitchen staff members, who looked furious as if they had a score to settle, entered to reprimand, or instead threaten, the class for vandalising and creating a mess. They had seen the actual culprits, but because this class was already notorious for being troublemakers, no teacher required any evidence to penalise them, as their reputation preceded them.

When the class heard the aunties shouting at them, they felt somewhat stunned and confused, pondering aloud.

"What did we do now?"

"Are you seriously going to ask that question after making a mess of the whole school?"

"You'll need to be a bit more specific."

"Your lot is full of it, and we will report you."

"Wait, first of all, that wasn't us, and you know you saw."

"Well, who do you think the principal and deputy principal will believe us or the vigilantes of the school?"

The poor 7th graders couldn't believe their ears as they stared at each other in awe.

"How about we tell them now, and let's find out?"

"Don't test us."

"If anything, you are treading on thin ice."

The aunties were furious and determined to pin this crime on 7c, fully aware that they had been unruly and would not accept this injustice without a fight, especially not from the aunties. Zazi remained as quiet as ever, her eyes darting from face to face, analysing and observing every expression. After a while, the aunties felt defeated as they stormed back to the kitchen, demanding never to see 7c again, while one of Zazi's classmates shouted, "Oh, but you will."

When the aunties heard Tando shout at the top of their lungs, they turned around and asked, "Who said that?" They wondered who it was.

"Who said what?"

"That!"

"You must be hallucinating."

They could not stomach these kids anymore, and with that said, they were gone. "Tando!!!" The whole class exhaled and laughed, surprised

"Sorry guys, it just came out"

They all laughed again

"It's alright; they were full of nonsense anyway."
"Thanks for having my back, guys."
"It's alright. We are all family here."

They all sat quietly as they debated the matter when Mrs Bolani walked in, prompting everyone to sit up straight and dash to their seats. "I heard you made a complete mess of the canteen," Mrs Bolani began, and the entire class suddenly found themselves unable to articulate words, clearing throats that had inexplicably gone dry.

"What, Ma'am?" They pretend to ask shockingly as if this was news to them

"The aunties came to report you guys, saying you vandalised the kitchen and then mocked them."

"Oh, Ma'am, we assure you we did no such thing. If anything, they merely accuse us and claim they would pin everything on us, given that we are already considered problematic. Therefore, it wouldn't take much for you to believe them."

"Oh, I see. Is that so?"

"Yes, ma'am!"

"Well, I'll talk to them, although why would they do such a thing?"

"No idea, that's what we asked when they saw who was responsible for all that, and they know very well which classes and which children were involved, yet they are blaming us instead."

The bell rang. It was time for the next period

"Ok then, you are dismissed; I'll have a word with the aunties."

"They also told us never to come to the kitchen again as they wouldn't serve us."

"Oh, trust me, they wouldn't dare."

As they made their way to the next class, another period had just begun, and they were heading to Mrs. Mfamana's class. As they walked in a straight line, she was seated at her desk, patiently waiting as if she had anticipated them for ages to share her thoughts. At that moment, it was evident that she, too, had heard the news. They quietly took their seats.

"Let's cut to the chase, shall we? What happened at the canteen?"

Zazi's eyes widened from corner to corner, and it felt as though the cat had stolen their voices; they breathed nothing but silence.

"I will not ask again, so better get to talking"

"Okay, well, that was not us."

"That did what?"

Made a mess in the kitchen or threw the food on the walls."

"Then how come I heard otherwise?"

"Well, they claimed they would inform the principal and deputy principal, and given that our reputation already precedes us, it wouldn't take much for anyone to believe them."

"How convenient"

"We are only telling the truth."

"Why should I believe you?"

"You wouldn't, but we are only answering your question, not trying to alter your mind, and we apologise for the inconvenience."

"Okay, aunties will have to deal with me instead."

"Huh?"

For a moment, they thought Mrs Mfamana was about to give them a good telling-off, but no, even she recognised how absurd the accusations were. She needed to hear their side of the story before unleashing her fury like Thor, the Lord of Thunder, on those aunties.

"I know you didn't do anything because as problematic as you are, it doesn't make you lunatics, and having me as your class teacher wouldn't dare."

"Well, we are just glad someone believes us."

"What did Mrs Bolani say about all this?"

"She said she would have a word with the aunties."

"Well then, I should go see her and you lot. I want you to be as silent as a mute."

"Yes, ma'am"

As she exited the room, her heels clicked against the floor as she walked out the door. The class took a deep breath, realising they had just dodged a bullet. Luck hasn't been on their side this particular year, as Zazi recalled how they all got punished because AKhona brought a taser to school and went around electrocuting pupils as a prank. In doing so, he mistakenly teased the wrong kid and got caught. He received 10 of the best while he fell on his knees, still stubborn and refusing to apologise. The bell rang as Zazi snapped out of her thoughts, and Thando dragged her to the next class with Mrs Duna, who taught them Social Sciences (History and Geography). She wasn't the best teacher but rather a raging lunatic. Definitely! Mrs Duna's class was in the same corridor as Mrs Mfamana's class. It was right next door but on the left. They entered, stood as she greeted them, and instructed them to take their seats.

"My homework!" she yelled, and before others could finish arguing, she said, "You didn't give us homework, ma'am, like every other day."

"This is not an open discussion but an order. Could you take out your books and open them? I want to see my homework completed."

Everyone decided to keep quiet and take out their books. Mrs. Duna was a different breed. She demanded respect, though she preferred to instil fear in her students' eyes. She thrived on the trembling that overtook her students when she regarded them, as they could barely meet her gaze before she cut them apart with her sharp words. So everyone placed their books on the table.

"If you know you didn't do my homework or didn't finish, come to stand here in front."

The class seemed to be still as if they hadn't heard

"I'll assume you didn't hear me, so I'll kindly repeat myself: if you haven't done your homework or finished it, come and stand behind me. If I find you seated, having not completed my work, you will regret it."

That said, many students—literally 90% of the class — jumped from their desks and to the front.

"Is that everybody?"

"Yes, ma'am"

"So if I were to go around now to those seated, would I find my work done and completed?"

"Yes, ma'am"

One more person quickly stood up and went to the front

"Okay, you! Okay, you don't tilt your head. I'm talking to you; get my pipe from Mrs Swazi."

As she pointed at Olivia, who was my desk mate, she quickly stood up

"Hurry, child, I don't have all day."

She ran and came back in a jiffy

"Here you go, ma'am"

"Go sit down."

Olivia sat down as Mrs Duna asked those standing at the front who had not done the homework and who had not finished. Those who had not done it were instructed to stand on the left, while those who had not completed it were asked to stand on the right.

"Now, what shall I do with you lot?"

"Forgive us", they pleaded.

"Forgive you? Most of you don't even bother to question my work every other day; therefore, I can't, and I ought to set an example. But as long as you can go and stand outside…"

As they hurriedly made their way outside, pushing one another

"Quietly"

"Sorry, ma'am." They all went outside, and Mrs Duna decided she could neither mark nor continue with that work as more than half the class hadn't completed it. Consequently, she moved on to a topic she had already begun. As usual, while teaching, she also posed questions and demanded answers, becoming frustrated whenever the class couldn't provide an explanation or one that she sought, even though she always preached, "It doesn't matter whether your answer is right or wrong as long as you answer; school is a place for mistakes."

Mocking and ridiculing the students when their answers were unsatisfactory, she looked at them with disgust and pity, saying, "You are foolish; anyone else?" Answering while seated was not an option, and remaining seated without being instructed was a significant issue. This was evident in the case of Hlumelo, who refrained from responding because he was weary of being mocked. He thought to himself, *what's the point?* This was the worst choice he could have made as she slowly approached him, asking, "What are you? Mute?"

Hamilton remained silent and just stared at her with his eyes

"Answer me, damn it!". She demanded, losing her patience and anger as the whole class watched her

The boy still wouldn't answer. She got tired of yelling

And started cussing and cursing at him

"You stupid idiotic minded and ugly thing"

She planned to provoke him, but Hlumelo wouldn't say a word. Next, Mrs Duna swung her arm, and her hand struck his face, pushing him backwards, but his desk caught her. The whole class was in awe as they gasped in shock, "OH MY GOODNESS!" everyone knew she had no right to do that; given how infuriated Hlumelo was, everyone thought he would retaliate, but instead, he grabbed his bag and packed his books, stood up, and marched towards the door. Mrs Duna looked even more angered.

"Where are you going?"

"Just let me go" he bagged

"I asked you a question."

"Please move"

"This is my class. Therefore, you can't just waltz in and out of here as you please."

"Well, you slapped me, so I have the right to report it, even if it means walking out as you speak."

"Okay, what do you want?" She pleaded

The whole class found that hilarious, thinking, "Not Mrs Duna trying to bribe a student after assaulting him."

"To call my father"

"Oh, but why?" her voice almost sounding lost and a bit shaken
"You slapped me; what do you think?"
"Well, students aren't allowed phones on the school premises."
"That's why I'm going to the principal's office."

He gently pushed her to the side, sick of arguing, as her delay tactics were in vain.

He walked out of the classroom, and suddenly, Mrs Duna was sweating, her hands shaking; I am reasonably sure she realised that she had just crossed a line as an educator that she had no business crossing. She took a handful of tissues from her desk and began wiping her face hastily and repeatedly. The class watched her march out of the room and head to the principal's office. Assuming we plead with the principal, this matter should be resolved internally. As she left, most of the class went mad and started narrating and debating the situation and how they wished Hlumelo had fought back. If it had been one of them, they would have slapped her back, and apparently, she does this all the time, often getting away with it because the students don't report her. However, everyone swore that this time around, she would definitely reap what she had sown.

The bell rang again; next class, we filed out, and on their way, bumped into 7e and 7c, who clearly could not wait to vent their frustrations. It seemed most of them had forgotten they had another class to attend. Mrs Duna slapping Hlumelo became the highlight of the day, and within moments, the whole school was buzzing about it. Meanwhile, Zazi was eager to get home, as the day had become overwhelming. The school was finally out. Zazi immediately dashed to her transport, wondering if Mrs Duna had slapped her. Would she have reported it? How would she have reacted? Would her grandparents entertain the matter? Her grandpa likely wouldn't have. By the time she arrived home, both her grandparents were there. She broke the news to them about what had happened at school, and surprisingly, her grandpa didn't see the issue with what he considered a fitting punishment from the educator. Zazi's grandma, being an educator herself, did not take it well, arguing that the teacher had no right to behave that way.

Meanwhile, her grandpa remarked that if she were to be hit by a teacher, she should never bother to mention it, as he had no time for nonsense and wouldn't entertain the issue. Sophie was quite shocked that her husband had said that, and she attempted to reason with him, "First of all, no teacher is meant to hit a child. It's against the law."
"Well then, no child should misbehave them."
"That's why there's an option to call in the guardians."

Zazi's ears had had enough, so she went to her room and immediately fell into a deep slumber. Days passed, and school became more intense as the weeks went by. It was the Afrikaans period. On their way to Mr Williams's class, they saw him walking out as they entered, his pace quicker than usual, staring straight ahead, not glancing sideways or uttering a word. They spent the entire lesson in his class, and he didn't return until the bell rang and the period ended. There was still no word as they passed him on the way out. Zazi wasn't sure what was wrong, but she knew Mr Williams was avoiding them, and she needed to find out why, as this couldn't continue with exams looming. Their next class was English with Mrs Wyngat. They entered and greeted her as she began teaching, despite a classmate who wouldn't stop talking. Her name was Joy. Joy was a very loud, tall, dark-skinned and slender girl with short hair who was bubbly, vocal, and outspoken. Disrespectful, she sometimes enjoyed ridiculing her fellow students, mocking teachers, and engaging in back-chatting.
"Excuse me, I'm trying to teach here. Do you mind ?"
"As a matter of fact, I do piss off," she replied, as the whole class turned their heads, thinking it was a slip of the tongue. Mrs Wyngat stepped closer and asked, "What did you just say to me?"
"I said piss off, what? Are you deaf?"
"Ok, missy, get out of my class"
"And if I don't?"
The whole class gasped with their jaws mopping the floor

"You will not speak to me like."

"Oh, but I just did."

"Get out!!!"

"Say I don't, then what?"

"This is my class."

"And I'm a student who has every right to be here, so if you don't have anything better to say, better get back to your job."

"Joy!!!" the rest of the class screamed. Given her excessive behaviour, this was jarring, even for Zazi's unruly classmates.

"Fine! I need some fresh air anyway," she said.

Standing up, she looked Mrs Wyngat straight and said, "Oh, don't cry. I was just playing."

And she stepped out, Mrs Wyngat feeling sentimental after being mocked and utterly embarrassed by a student. She ran out of the classroom in tears, while some students found it funny and weak. Meanwhile, Zazi couldn't be more disgusted. She couldn't comprehend how her classmates found this amusing. The period ended. Mrs Wyngat still hadn't returned, and Zazi was worried about the repercussions this might cause, with her and everyone else in the class implicated, whether guilty or not. First, it was the incident with Mrs Duna, then Mr Williams, who refused to teach them because her classmates were unruly, and now this is the case with Mrs Wyngat, who also would not be teaching them afterwards. As Zazi's mind began to race, she thought, what if they failed in their behaviour? As much as she wouldn't blame the teachers, it still wouldn't be fair, but neither was what her classmates did to the teachers.

She couldn't help but worry. English was the last period of the day, and Zazi was starving from frustration after buying fish and chips from street vendors outside the schoolyard. She got into her transport and headed home, with Mr Dambuza dropping her off at the front gate as usual. As was her routine, upon arriving home from school, she had to teach Anton English, which was most effectively done through reading, although he preferred listening and watching instead. Conversely, Amanda didn't want to be taught; she wanted Zazi to complete her homework and assignments for her as if Zazi didn't already have enough on her plate with her 7th-grade work. On top of that, she had to teach an 8th grader and handle a 9th grader's workload for Amanda, who barely lifted a finger. Zazi didn't mind taking on all the work, but she worried about how she would manage during exams since she wouldn't be there to write them on her behalf…

Twelve

Facing the Ruins

"To rebuild yourself, you must first face the ruins."
"Healing begins when you stop running from the pain and start uncovering the pieces of yourself hidden beneath it."

There was to be a fundraiser called SUMMER SPLASJ. The school held these types of fundraisers every year. Typically, the 7th graders of Louis Rex would go camping before the end of the year, but according to the teachers, they wouldn't have one because they were unruly. As the year drew to a close, they discovered it was due to the school lacking funds, hence the numerous fundraising events. Yet, for some reason, they still couldn't manage the finances.

This summer splash was meant to be a carnival-like festival with a pool. It was Friday, and letters had already been sent on Mondays to inform the parents and request money for the goodies that the school would sell and the tickets to the shows. However, Zazi detested fundraisers, not due to the funding, but because they usually resulted in more chaos than usual. Finally, Friday arrived, and they had to dress casually, which wasn't new, as that was an every Friday tradition accompanied by an R2 fee.

The year had drawn to a close, and although the teachers were fully occupied with the 7th graders, this felt like a farewell designed for them to celebrate with the entire school. It was a sunny, tranquil day. The teachers had organised a plastic pool that needed pumping before adding water and diving in. The children had brought their swimming gear. There were swings and merry-go-rounds, creating an atmosphere reminiscent of a play park. The teachers had set up a braai stand selling hot dogs, burgers, and soft drinks. Of course, there was also the haunted house, where the teachers dressed up and painted themselves as if it were a Halloween party, decorating the entire classroom with owl statues and coffins; it resembled a place where Dracula would dwell.

The house was meant to provide thrill and gore; however, Zazi couldn't help but find it ridiculous for a child who had grown up watching horror films and murder documentaries. She felt the teachers could have done more, yet all the learners were screaming and clinging to her shirt as if they were about to be eviscerated. She realised she was overreacting as she couldn't comprehend what was frightening about it, and of course, she detested noise; it resembled the worst scene from a horror film. Throughout the day, she spent her time reminiscing about the year, considering how her peers were rushing into things. She never understood why they were so eager to fall in love and in such a hurry to grow up. It was all rather creepy, yet she was deemed the weirdo for pointing it out.

At least she and her friends were still cool. Olivia was dating Zulu, who had moved from KZN to here only this year. His name was Siyakholwa Khumalo. He was dark-skinned and short—really dark, as in Shaka Zulu dark—not skinny or tall, though he had the physique of a rugby player. Then there was Sivuyile, whom Zazi didn't know much about except that he was Bridgette's childhood friend. He was tall, skinny, and light-skinned but not as light as Bridgette. Sivuyile had a crush on Bridgette and had confided in Zazi, asking for her advice as he didn't know how to tell her, although Bridgette already knew; it was so apparent that not even a blind man would miss it. The only problem was that Bridgette didn't feel the same, nor did she want to date.

Although Zazi endeavoured to be a good friend and persuade Bridgette to give Sivuyile a chance, it didn't work out. The thought of Sivuyile repulsed Bridgette, but not all was lost, as Sivuyile ended up with Thandolwethu Lunda. Then there was Andiswe Tintelo, the most beautiful girl in our year. She was dark-skinned, impeccably neat, and she never wore socks, only stockings. Well, most of the girls did. She had the perfect face and figure. She was dating Asakhe Nikane (Ace), the cleverest in school, as he had more certificates than anyone except Alive Sifuba. Ace also happened to be one of the top three biggest guys in school, although Zazi always thought Brandon was more attractive. Oh, and of course, there were Tania Philips and Ikho, the school's most famous couple. Tania was a petite, almost Indian-looking coloured girl who dated this tall, dark, handsome young man known as the Equator, given his height. Although Ikho never truly liked Tania, he had his sights set on this rather dashing young lady, Linamandla Nqoba (Lina), who was fair-skinned and one of the most gorgeous girls in school, was quiet, kept to herself, got along with everyone, and was the sweetest, including Zazi. She wasn't loud and didn't curse; she had the purest of hearts.

Last but not least, the second most popular couple, Gift Naidoo, wasn't the most handsome chap but was a wealthy lad, a cheese boy who occasionally arrived at school in his father's Porsche. The gift was dating Siyamthanda Godana, known as Getty. Another pretty girl was the lightest-skinned student the school had to offer and got on well with everyone, of course. She was the sweetest until you crossed her, as she always got into fights. Then, of course, there was Sothemba Tom, the most attractive guy in school whom every girl desired, including Getty, Andiswe, and the brightest girls in school, Alive and Mbali. Slindokuhle, well, except for Tania, Linamandla, and Zazi. Lima was too focused on her studies to concern herself with boys, whilst Zazi, on the other hand, was never interested. Sothemba was quite the heartthrob.

He never actually dated anyone, but every girl wanted to kiss, date, and do everything with him, yet he was never the dating type.

Amahle, the rugby player who wasn't dating anyone, and his foolish friends, Musa and Akhona. Amahle played rugby, as did Akhona. The primary difference was that rugby was the only thing Amahle Mafuta excelled at or paid any attention to, alongside Phaphama Peter. You could tell Phaphama was a rugby player; the boy was built for it and spent considerable time in the gym. He lived in the shadow of his brother, who was now in high school but also a rugby player and an A student. However, unlike Keagon, he didn't possess the same intellect as his twin brother, Brandon, and was consequently ridiculed. Returning to the fundraiser, Zazi was roaming the school grounds with Tando, as everyone else had disappeared into whatever direction the wind blew. Suddenly, they encountered Bridgette, who appeared more hyper than usual as she blurted out something unprovoked while holding a school bottle that Zazi would have thought contained juice.

"I'm getting wasted."

"Wait, what?"

"Yes, you want to have a taste?"

Zazi looked around simultaneously and didn't eat, but Bridgette didn't appear to be taking no for an answer.

"You are joking, right?"

"No, but you are welcome to have a taste."

As she grabbed her head, tilted it and shoved the bottle down her throat, she almost threw up as she started choking and coughing, barely even breathing.

"Bridgette! Have you lost your mind?"

"Relax, sweetie. Look around. Everyone's getting drunk or high, loosen up."

She scanned the school grounds, unable to believe her eyes. Joy and her mates were carrying wine bottles and sacks. Furious with Bridgette, Zazi chose to storm off, dragging poor Tando along as if she could erase the thoughts swirling in her mind: What if she got caught? What if she were expelled?

Suspended? Or had her grandparents been called in? Her grandad wouldn't hesitate to cause a scene before the teachers.

Tando: hey, was that alcohol

Zazi: Honestly, I can't believe Bridgette shoved it down my throat

Tando: look! Bridgette wasn't joking. People are wasted

Zazi: no kidding

Asakhe, Gift, Shona, Xavier, and the other boys stood in the sun before Mr Hattrick's class, smoking weed as if they were invisible. They were right by the braai stands with Mr Williams, Mr Miller, Mr Soekdien, and Mr Hartnick opposite them, yet they went unnoticed. Zazi and Tando were minding their own business when Mrs Jansen came charging like a thought. It seemed that some people just got it.

"Are you lot drinking here?"

"No, ma'am"

"Really? Then what's in that bottle?"

"Water Juffrou"

"So you are not drunk?"

"No, ma'am"

As they couldn't stop laughing, it must have been the cannabis.

"Alright, stand on one leg. Let's see."

They all stood on one leg with their arms in the air for approximately 5 minutes.

"You can stop now."

"Ok, but what did we do?"

How classic of Asakhe to act lost

"Well, we just found out that the lot of you are drunk, so we are checking for all those who were drinking."

After hearing that Zazi's heart had almost stopped, did Bridgette get caught saying she was drinking as well? Or was it someone else? A laugh suddenly annoyed her out of her thoughts.

"What's wrong with you?"

"Nothing, why?" Zazi asked

"You look dead."

"Huh?"

"Your skin is pale, and you are all sweaty."

"Oh, that.."

"What? Don't tell me Mrs Jansen scared you."

"No, no, why would she?"

Barely able to keep a straight face or form a sentence, Bridgette suddenly jumped from behind, nearly wetting herself.

"boo!"

"What the hell?"

"Have you guys seen Mrs Jansen?"

Tando: she just passed here…

Zazi: why?

Bridgette: well, she wants a list of all those who were drinking and smoking

Tando: and?

Zazi: why are you telling us?

Bridgette: Well, I was drinking too, and so were my friends, including you

Tando: who?

Zazi: you must be out of your mind

Bridgette: we'll see

Zazi blinked once, and Bridgette had vanished. She felt the walls closing in on her, suddenly sweating as the others were dragged to the office and pointed out.

"You were drinking too; come along."

"Says who?"

"Bridgette"

"Bridgette is full of it; where is she? I'll deal with her."

Zazi, feeling annoyed, attempted to locate Bridgette. Before making any progress, she spotted Tania dangling from Mr Hartnick's window.

"Tania, get out; you can't use the window."

"But I want to sleep", she muttered.

"Well, use the door, not the window. If they catch you, you'll also be sent to the office."

The others warned
"Where's Ikho? Where's my man?"
"At the office."
"With Asakhe and the others"

As she continued to breach the window, the other students tried to catch her, while some wanted to push her back inside. Zazi, however, was shocked. She honestly could not believe her eyes. She couldn't fathom how a young scholar even managed to get alcohol and consume it within the school premises. "Ami, the only one trying not to get expelled from this school?" she screamed internally. Tania finally managed to clamber out of the window as the others assisted, catching sight of her determination to get her "man" after someone shouted, "They are expelling Ikho."

They wouldn't dare! "She rushed to the principal's office, and as the others followed suit, she returned to recount and gossip about how she had wet herself and made a scene in the office. Poor Ikho was so embarrassed.

"Where's Ikho? Where's my man?"

He was unaware of whether the teachers or the principal himself were present. "Ikho wasn't drinking; I was. As you can see, he is sober. You. You should let him go so that we can go and sleep."

The gossip continued. Zazi had heard enough and even forgot she was looking for Bridgette. Since she wasn't dragged to the office, she let it go. The bell rang, signalling that school was out, and they all hurried to the school gate. Zazi's transport hadn't arrived yet, so she and Tando left. Victoria had sent her money to buy the sneakers she wanted, which she got through her grandpa. Therefore, she asked Tando to accompany her to the mall. They walked, having fun along the way. They started at Nonesi Mall. After checking out all the shops, Zazi decided to buy the sneakers at Studio 808. They left the mall and went to the other one near the casino at Pick 'n Pay. They cracked jokes and poked fun at some people. Zazi bought snacks at the

R5 store, then crossed over to Debonairs Pizza, purchased some pizza and cool drinks, and sat down to eat. Tando felt guilty that she wasn't paying for anything and was just eating, although Zazi reassured her that it was fine. Afterwards, they planned to go to boxing if it was still early and they weren't returning to school. Zazi accompanied Tando to the taxi rank, gave her taxi fare, and then walked home. She had learned the way home from travelling to school every day, even if it was by car.

Thirteen

Knowing Thyself

"Knowing yourself is the greatest victory, for it signifies that you have endured everything that sought to break you."

"To know yourself is not merely to discover the pieces—but to embrace them, scars and all, and to forge something complete."

It was now exam time, the end of the year in the school calendar, and it felt almost like the end of the game just as Zazi walked into her class. Everyone gave her odd looks and stares, and her aversion to attention made it overwhelming. She felt creeped out and was drowning in anxiety. Suddenly, this rather forward girl, who had never so much as breathed next to Zazi in the two years she had been at Louis Rex, approached and smiled at her, though the smile was condescending, leaving Zazi to wonder what she had done this time. Then, a question jolted her from her frozen state: "Is it true you have a crush on Brandon?"

"What? Who said that?".

How could she even know? Where did she, even as she has never told anyone about this secret of hers

"He did"

"Wait, he knows that? How did he?"
"So you do have a crush on him?"
"What's it to you?"
"Nothing. I am just a messenger."
"Who's the messenger? What for?"
"Brandon"
"What?"
"He doesn't like you, he never has, never will"
"Why didn't he just say that himself?"
"He thought it easier."
"You are not even friends."
"Exactly why he sent me."
"Doesn't make sense."
"Oh well, I'll let him know."

She fled like the wind, while Zazi, on the other hand, was overcome with embarrassment as she hastily untied her tie from her neck and undid the first few buttons of her shirt. I tried to make sense of the entire situation, but I couldn't conclude. As for how Thandokazi would know any of this, she had never told anyone about the well, except, of course, Olivia, who then admitted that she too adored Brandon, thereby confessing that she would let Zazi have him since they were friends and she had mentioned it first. Even though Zazi was never naive, she knew she was lying, and a guy like Brandon would never fancy a girl like her. He was smart, clever, handsome—the hottest boy in school, a decent chap, and a soccer player. The most non-scandalous guy there was in the school, or so she thought. She stood there in awe as peers from other classes came to ask her questions one by one, and for the first time, people noticed her existence, but she wished she could have crawled back into her limbo, her invisible self, where no one recognised her. "You? Have a crush on Brandon?"

"Ew! No wonder he's so offended." As they giggled, SBS felt distraught. She turned her head as tears filled her eyes, scanned the room, and attempted to locate her "friends" but had no luck. Tandokazi returned to deliver the news. One could tell from the expression on her face that she relished this entire charade.

"Brandon says you should take that crush of yours and shove it up your arse because you and he could never happen, and to think he treated you as a friend; you disgust him…"

"What? I don't understand where's all of this coming from?".

"Brandon, whom else?"

"That doesn't sound like him; I know him. He wouldn't say that."

"You don't know him as well as you would like to; I'll tell him you said that"

"Wait, can I talk to him?"

"Sweetie, if he wanted to talk to you, he would tell you all this instead of me."

"I don't believe you."

"Being delusional won't save you this time."

Zazi was shattered to the core. How could the one guy she thought was the most decent treat her like this? Of course, she knew he would never go for her, but did he have to taunt her like this? What had she done to deserve such treatment? As her whole class watched her crushed, humiliated, and embarrassed, trying to hold back her tears while Thandokazi returned with murder in her eyes, Zazi was determined to destroy her.

"Brandon says believe whatever you wish, but don't you dare for a second think you know him; the big man has been trying to rid himself of you for months, but you've clung to him like a nail to wood."

"He did? I mean, I didn't mean to."

She struggled to fight back tears and swallow her words, explaining and apologising that she never intended to like him more than she ought. Tears streamed down her face, one after the other. Her vision was nearly blurry, but she could still see Tandokazi smiling. She could hear the amazement and amusement in her voice at the sight of her crying. Yet, she couldn't understand why Brandon's words hurt her so profoundly or why she was even crying.

"I would kill myself if I were… Didn't mean to what exactly? Be stupid enough to think that a guy like that would ever like a girl like you? I'm sure you even forced the friendship, but he was too much of a guy to tell you no."

Suddenly, flashbacks began to overwhelm her, recalling times when Brandon would turn away from her as if he didn't want to engage in conversation, appearing quite annoyed. At times, he would pull away, becoming moody and refusing to include her in discussions, opting instead to converse with everyone else. Occasionally, he even stopped socialising with the group during breaks and would choose to play football with some lads she typically didn't associate with.

Did she suffocate him? Did she push him away? Does he now hate her? Does that mean he doesn't even want to be friends with her? With all that, what did that mean for their friendship? After seeing how she had shattered Zazi's world. Thandokazi could see the disbelief and the wishing it was just a bad dream on Zazi's face, so she asked, "What? You still don't believe me? Legs go" As she dragged her by the arm, all the grade 7 classes watched as Zazi tried to stop her. "What? You wanted to see him, didn't you? Talk to him? Ask him why. Well, now's your chance" She was so weak within every part of her limbs that she couldn't even say no, let alone unhand herself from Thandokazi's grip as she tried to wipe her tears and runny nose with the edge of her jersey. She could hear the laughter almost bursting her eardrums, the stares nearly ripping her head from her throat.

She felt Thabdokazi's grip loosen from her arm, and suddenly, she found herself standing alone. Opening her eyes, she realised she had been left to the wolves to be finished off by the vultures waiting to complete their feasting. The stares were so unhinged that she wanted to cover her face and erase this day. Suddenly, she spotted him with his hands in his pockets, facing the other way, when that fine back turned as someone tapped his shoulder and probably whispered in his ear, "Looks like you're in trouble," as his face slowly turned. His eyes met hers, and she could finally breathe. Yet then she remembered all those messages Thandokazi had sent, claiming they were from him, and suddenly she was blinded by sadness and overwhelmed; she felt herself cringe at the thought before blurting out, "What did I ever do to you?"

"What? What are you talking about?"

"You sending Tandokazi to come and deliver messages with you mocking and insulting me."

"Zazi, you are not making sense. I would never do that, plus why would I do that?"

"But but…Tandokazi said …"

"And you believe her? So that's why you are here accusing me and looking like this …"

"I'm sorry," she whispered, realising that everyone had gone quiet and was listening to them as she ran off in shame, thinking that, like in the movies, he would run after her as she entered the girls' toilet and buried herself in the sink to wash away the feeling of patheticness. She couldn't believe how gullible and weak she felt today and how Thabdokazi manipulated her like that. She cried in front of the entire school, feeling embarrassed and humiliated, yet she could still withstand the laughter. She remembered the expressions on everyone's faces as they laughed, looked at her, and gossiped.

She wiped her face and returned to her desk in class; she hadn't seen a single teacher since she arrived at school that day. She wondered where they might be and where her so-called friends were in her time of need. Returning to her seat, she folded her arms, laid them on the desk, and buried her face. Hearing all the whispers and jokes directed at her, she resolved to act as if she couldn't hear any of it. With a heavy heart, she fell asleep amidst all that white noise.

The school bell rang. She must have been really out of it, as someone woke her by shaking her. "School's out," he whispered before disappearing. She awoke in an empty classroom, unsure how to face everyone outside again. Eventually, she stepped outside, got into her transport, and shut the door just as she heard a familiar voice calling her name at least twice. "Zazi, Zazi, wait!" So now he suddenly wanted to talk to her, and although she could feel him running towards her, she climbed into her transport without so much as a greeting. She simply stared out the window, replaying today's incident repeatedly.

I thought about how she could ever go back to school after that. Yes, it's exams; they will just write and go home, but she can't. Unlike what happened today, she knew neither could the rest of the school. At the same time, she wondered what Brandon could have wanted, and although she still liked him, she just couldn't bring herself to talk to anyone just yet. Maybe he had run after her when she needed him to. She probably would have gotten over it, and so would everyone else, to prove his argument of "I did say that." So much for friendship, huh? she thought as the car drove off.

I mean, he couldn't even defend her. He just stood there looking at her as if she were mad, suggesting she was making things up, and how maybe she shouldn't have known, and perhaps she should have. She got home, and at this point, she couldn't care less about whose turn it was to cook and clean. She just needed to stop thinking and stop hurting. So, as soon as she got home, she threw her bag on the floor, didn't even take off her uniform, and just got into bed, falling into a deep slumber. The weekend passed, and she had to return to school like a strong soldier as if it were the last day of the exam and her parcel from Victoria had arrived.

The farewell was just around the corner as she avoided Branding and everyone else. Every day leading up to it, she would go to school, take exams, and come straight home without speaking to anyone, so attending the farewell felt like a step backwards she was unprepared for. On the farewell day, Zazi bathed and rummaged through her clothes in Victoria, deciding what to wear. Ultimately, she chose to wear her trousers, although uncertain about what to do with her hair, which resembled steel wool and had just been combed. She was waiting for her grandpa to pick her up, but he took his time returning from work, so she had to ask the tenants living in the flat at the back, who had no problem giving her a lift.

When she arrived, she realised how hideous she looked compared to her peers, who were dropped off in extravagant cars, not to mention their stylish outfits and chauffeurs who appeared to fit the part. Zazi felt embarrassed to leave the car, but she did because she was already there. She watched her peers from her table, looking like a lost puppy as she slowly picked at what was on her plate. Without realising how quickly time had passed, she saw her grandpa at the door and realised it was time to leave.

Epilogue

The wind carried a familiar scent as Zazi stood at the hill overlooking her grandparents' house. It was the same breeze that had once mocked her, swirling around her as she ran from her pain. But today, it felt different. Softer. Almost like an embrace.

She let her gaze sweep across the town she had once tried to escape. The dust, the winding roads, and the faint sound of distant laughter were still here, but something had changed. No, it wasn't Queenstown. It was her.

For years, Zazi had pondered whether she would ever discover her true self. As a young girl, she had prayed for answers, uncertain whether they would come from her absent mother, the grandparents who had tried but sometimes struggled, or the mirror that reflected only fragments of her identity.

But now, she realized something she wished her younger self had known: the answers were never out there. They were within her all along.

She thought of the nights she had cried in silence, terrified of the darkness that surrounded her. She remembered Byron's cruelty, her mother's betrayal, and the faces of those who stood by while her world fell apart. She had hated them once. She had hated herself more.

And yet, here she stood. Her fingers brushed the pendant around her neck—

the one her grandmother had given her as a child. It had meant nothing to her then, just another token in a life where love felt transactional. But now, it was different. The weight of it felt like an anchor, grounding her. It reminded her of the promise she made to herself not long ago: *to live, rebuild, and know herself.*

Zazi turned her face to the sky, letting the sunlight warm her skin. She had spent years running, searching for someone to love her enough to fix her. But she didn't need fixing anymore. She had stitched her wounds, one painful thread at a time.

"Mom," she whispered into the wind, not with anger but with release. "I forgive you."

The words startled her. She hadn't planned to say them, but they felt right, not for her mother's sake but for her own. Letting go of the bitterness felt like shedding a heavy coat she had outgrown.

As she returned to the house, she heard laughter—the twins, Amanda and Anton, teasing each other. She had grown to cherish this sound. Her grandmother's voice followed, sharp but loving, as she scolded them to behave.

Zazi stopped at the door and looked back one last time.

This town, this family, this life had shaped her, broken her, and made her whole again. She wasn't the girl she used to be. She wasn't afraid of the darkness anymore.

"Zazi," her grandmother called from inside. "Lunch is ready."

She smiled, her heart lighter than it had ever been.

Her story wasn't over. The girl who had once been lost had found herself. And now, she was ready to write her next chapter.

About the Author

Awonke Zoya is a multi-talented South African artist from the Eastern Cape who is celebrated for her contributions to music, dance, and visual arts. Born and raised in a small town, Awonke's early life was defined by her passion for dancing, which garnered recognition within her family and community. Despite her shyness, she began drawing and sketching in the second grade, drawing inspiration from her creative family members.

After her mother left in 2006, Awonke was raised in a Christian household by her grandparents. In 2007, she moved from Lady Frere to Queenstown. Her uncle's skills as a sketch artist and DJ, along with her aunt's diverse talents as a sound engineer, sketch artist, vocalist, rapper, and writer, greatly influenced her artistic development. She credits them for her artistic inclinations, apart from her dancing talent.

Awonke penned her first poem, "Forgotten," and her inaugural rap, "22," in 2015 upon returning from Cape Town. Her musical journey commenced with the song "Tears of a Broken Heart," produced by Lucas. In 2021, Awonke wrote, recorded, and mastered her debut project, "The Truth Skips Naked EP," which she uploaded to Audiomack.com. She initially performed under the stage name Raven A Zoya before changing it to Aeza in 2022. During this period, Awonke also continued creating dance videos and performing at various clubs, gaining further recognition through a radio interview on Vukani FM in Queenstown.

In 2023, Awonke joined Amaka Studio and launched her channel, showcasing her dancing, drawings, poetry, and songs. Her dedication and talent earned her the titles of Creator of the Month in March and Creator of the Year in December 2023. Awonke Zoya continues to explore and share her diverse artistic expressions, captivating audiences with her heartfelt creativity.

You can connect with me on:
- https://vip.dadyminds.org/author-azoya